T0113423

Praise for *Approximately Heaven*

"What Whorton does so well here is to re-create in pitch-perfect tones a particularly endearing form of male banter, in which the participants give each other enormous grief and say absolutely hilarious things while remaining stone-faced. For readers who like their humor on the droll side and their dialogue delivered deadpan."

—*Booklist*

"In this impressive debut novel, Whorton exhibits a dead-on ear for dialogue. The blue collar, work-hard-for-every-dollar Tennesseans he portrays with gentle humor are endearing even when they're behaving in politically incorrect and less-than-reasonable fashion."

—*BookPage*

"Narrating this funny, stellar first novel is one of the most infuriating losers you'll ever meet on a page. Whorton conjures through close observation a hilariously absurd world that holds, just possibly, the keys to its own salvation. Amid the absurdity, you can feel the hope."

—*The Tennessean*

"Don Brush is a great character, so real you feel you know him. His voice is wry, full of that self-deprecating tone that so many country storytellers use to hilarious effect."

—*The Baton Rouge Advocate*

"These two [characters] resemble a hard-drinking, working-class version of Don Quixote and Sancho Panza. Hilarious and poignant."

—*The Atlanta Journal-Constitution*

"*Approximately Heaven* is a splendid book by a fine new writer, subtle as few books are these days, but just like our lives—all nuance and intimacy. Whorton writes with delicacy and thought, and great wry humor. You'll love this funny, touching tale of charming and rotten misbehavior. A brilliant debut novel by a singularly gifted writer."

—Frederick Barthelme, author of *Moon Deluxe*

"A jim-dandy first novel: James Whorton's road-rambling, beer-guzzling, lost-souled rednecks are good narrative company indeed."

—John Barth, author of *The Sot-Weed Factor*

"A bright, lively debut by a writer with the skills to tell a solid, interesting story with a wide range of emotions, from humor to tenderness to something approximating, in such a quirky lead character, sorrow, though in the novel humor rules. Fast paced, often hilarious, always readable, and at times, through the clipped actions and sprightly down-home dialogue, thoroughly exhilarating. To those who thought minimalism in fiction was moribund, think again; Whorton, in *Approximately Heaven*, gives it a fresh and revitalizing shot in the arm."

—Stephen Dixon, author of *I.*

"While it's easy to be impressed with Whorton's technical skills . . . more impressive is his ability to get inside the mind of his hero with a minimum of excess. . . . From a deadpan prose style that captures Don's character perfectly, what emerges is a story of attempted redemption without the gushy sentimentality that usually accompanies that sort of book. Instead, Whorton's first novel is finely written and humorous, a compassionate but authentic look inside a struggling heart."

—*Nashville Scene*

"*Approximately Heaven* might be depressing stuff if it wasn't such a wildly funny and inventive portrayal of a particular man's sudden head-on with despair. . . . Whorton shows . . . with deadpan perfection how [a] simple man can be broken down over the course of many days and six-packs, then receive a second chance at life."

—*Southern Currents*

"An entertaining first novel. Whorton has created characters who, amid conversations about engines and sex and amid beer-drinking bouts and efforts to dodge responsibility, seek answers to the fundamental questions about life and who often discover their better selves in the process."

—*Lexington Herald-Leader*

Approximately Heaven

JAMES WHORTON, JR.

FREE PRESS

NEW YORK   LONDON   TORONTO   SYDNEY

fP

FREE PRESS
A Division of Simon & Schuster, Inc.
1230 Avenue of the Americas
New York, NY 10020

First Free Press trade paperback edition 2005

FREE PRESS and colophon are
trademarks of Simon & Schuster, Inc.

For information about special discounts for bulk purchases,
please contact Simon & Schuster Special Sales:
1-800-456-6798 or business@simonandschuster.com

Book design by Ellen R. Sasahara

Manufactured in the United States of America

1   3   5   7   9   10   8   6   4   2

The Library of Congress has catalogued the hardcover edition as follows:
Whorton, James, 1967–
Approximately heaven / James Whorton, Jr.
p. cm.
1. Mississippi—Fiction. 2. Tennessee—Fiction. I. Title.
PS3623.H6A85 2003
813'.6—dc21   2003048305
ISBN 0-7432-4446-X
ISBN 0-7432-4447-8 (Pbk)
ISBN 978-0-7432-4447-3

To Kathryn

Approximately
Heaven

1

IT WAS A SATURDAY MORNING and I was up early and on the front porch, getting ready to slice a tomato and eat it. The dog was looking up at me like he wanted some and I reminded him, "You don't like tomatoes."

I had heard nothing from Mary all morning. I concluded she must be sleeping in, so when she finally came downstairs and stepped out on the porch, I thought it would be good fun to provoke her a little. I told her she ought not to lie in bed so late, because it made her eyes puffy as though she had been crying.

"I wasn't lying in bed," she said. "I was packing."

"Packing?"

"I'm moving out, Don," she said.

I had not expected this. I knew there were certain aspects of things that she was not happy about, but I did not know we had reached an emergency stage. I said, "Mary, wait and let's talk about this." She shook her head no and said she had already thought it through and wasn't changing her mind. I said indignantly, "But I haven't thought it through."

"You don't have to think it through," she said. "I'm leaving, and that's it."

I studied her face, trying to understand what was happening, and my indignation began to wilt when I noticed how her jaw jutted, as I had seen it do many times before when she had made up her mind to get through some chore that she was dreading. Two things occurred to me: one that she was serious, and two that I loved her more than I knew what to do with.

I began to fall apart and believe that she was right and must go. Here was Mary, my wife of seven years, an attractive person with her sharp, serious eyes, and as smart as anybody, and tough, and at times humorous, and simply admirable in all respects. In contrast, here I was, a person of ordinary talents, at present unemployed, and not especially ambitious to improve, and really not mindful of anything in the world on that morning outside of my tomato that I had been planning to eat, and my knife that I had planned to slice it with. I had found the knife to be slightly dull, and so my whetstone was there too on the table like an emblem of my inability to get on with things.

I told Mary that she was completely right and something had to change. She deserved better, and I was the one at fault. Whatever would make her happy was what we needed to do next, I said. Looking back, I would call this a moment of pure selflessness on my part, except that it was only a moment, which makes me question its purity.

Mary sat down with me at the table. It was a former cable spool and she had polyurethaned the top of it. She pulled off her glasses and wiped them with the paper towel that my tomato had been resting on. Without her glasses she looks very vulnerable.

"I want you to be happy," I said.

"So do I."

"I won't be happy if you're not happy," I said. "I love you, and so therefore I want whatever is best for you."

She considered that and smiled. She put her glasses back on. She said, "But that's not really true, Don."

I said, "Well I want it to be true, and I intend for it to be true in the future. If you're not happy, I'm not happy. That's the program."

"I'm seeing a lawyer on Monday," she said.

"A lawyer? What for?"

There was more staring at each other now.

I said, "Look. I thought you were talking about moving out temporarily. That's what you just said, I think. Monday's a little abrupt to be seeing a lawyer, Mary."

She didn't speak. I stood up. I looked at the top of her head by the part in her hair, where there was a small stubbly spot. I had dropped a blob of SeamerMate in her hair when she was helping me with the gutter, and it'd had to be cut out with scissors. It was a small thing that would not have been very noticeable, had you not known where it was and had you not been standing directly over her head. There were so many reasons why I loved her! I reached to touch the stubbly spot, and she got up and went into the house.

"Monday is too soon to see a lawyer!" I said.

I followed her upstairs and saw her open bag on the bed with her clothes folded in it. It was only her overnight bag. She stood at the clothes rack by the wall. Her hanging clothes were on this rack made of pipe because we were remodeling, and I had torn out the closets upstairs. She pulled out a suit of hers and said, "Where is the hanging bag?"

"I don't know where it is," I said. "Somewhere."

She spun around and knocked her bare foot on the corner of a computer that was sitting in the floor beside the bed. The computer had not been plugged in for a couple of years. It was an old desktop computer from when they were still making all the cases out of metal. Mary swore and picked up her foot, and I took the suit from her.

I put my hand on her shoulder to steady her, and with my other hand I hung her suit back on the end of the rack. "You can leave this here for the time being," I said.

"My foot is bleeding," she said, and she went downstairs.

I looked at her bag on the bed, and something happened. I became alarmed and also distracted. It was panic. I picked through the clothes in the bag to see what all she was taking with her, and I wondered if she had a damned boyfriend. I went downstairs to the bathroom, where she was getting a Band-Aid. I said, "Have you got a boyfriend?"

"No."

"Let me move out, and you stay here in the house," I said.

"You can forget that idea," she said. "This house is making me batty."

She went to throw the Band-Aid wrapper away, but the wastebasket was crammed full. She shook the wrapper at me and then flung it. It fluttered sideways into the tub.

"I'm fed up!" she said.

"If the house is the problem, we can fix that," I said.

"Get out of the doorway, please!"

"Look here," I said. I ran up the stairs and into the bedroom, and in one move I lifted the computer, monitor, and keyboard in a stack from the carpet. I carried them downstairs. This wasn't an easy feat.

"Look, I'm throwing this out," I said. I got the door open and carried the computer outside, and I set it in the back of my truck. Then I went back inside the house, looking for more.

"I wish you had thrown that computer out a long time ago," Mary said.

"I know it," I said. I ran upstairs and started the vacuum.

Mary came up and told me to stop vacuuming. I pretended not to hear her. She went back down the stairs, and I unpacked her bag and put her clothes back in the dresser while the vacuum was running.

I paused to consider the carpet. It was striped in shades of purple, blue, and magenta. It wasn't a nice choice, and it had not been professionally installed. It had come with the house. Also, I noticed, the bed sagged, and the headboard did not line up with the windowsill because of a slope in the floor. One pane in the bottom sash of the window was cracked and had been repaired by me some time ago with a yellowish piece of strapping tape. It occurred to me that if I honestly wanted to be kind to my wife, I would encourage her to spend a few nights in a nice motel room.

That troubled me, because I did want to be kind. But what I wanted even more than that was for her to not leave me, ever. And I had the feeling, the more I paused and considered my surroundings, that if she once made the break and left this house, it would be very hard to ever talk her back into it. The house had many problems, entirely apart from the people who lived in it. Outside of the house it was a big world, and a person with my wife's merits would soon find new challenges and ways to spend time with more interesting people than myself. I would be left alone in the house then, with the carpet and without Mary.

I vacuumed. I tidied all the boxes of our stuff as well as possible—they were boxes that had not been unpacked in two years—and I gathered some scraps of lumber that had been lying about upstairs. After calling a warning, I tossed them from the window into the grass. I had been meaning to do this for weeks.

I ran back down the stairs and past Mary, who was sitting

on the sofa in her silent Indian Chief mode, holding the cat. I
ran out the front door and moved all the lumber from where it
had landed in the yard to the barn across the road. I was care-
ful not to block the lawn mowers, but otherwise I was just
adding junk to the pile that already included sheets of roof
metal and parts of broken farm implements from before our
time. It was a hazard but now was not the time to worry about
it. I strode back into the house and washed the dishes. I got a
headache. We were out of aspirin, so I took a beer from the
fridge and drank it at the sink, though it was earlier in the day
than I would normally have a beer. It was about ten, I guess.

I heard Mary on the stairs, and then I heard her walking
above me and then walking back and stepping down the stairs
again. She came into the kitchen. "Where are my clothes?" she
said. "What did you do with the clothes that were in my bag?"

"I put them away," I said. "I thought you were staying
now."

"I never said I was staying."

"Well, stay, and I'll go."

"No, I'm going," she said. She ran back upstairs, and I heard
her pulling open dresser drawers.

I went out to my truck and left.

2

I DROVE TO THE LOCAL DUMP. This was in Washington County, Tennessee, and we didn't have garbage pickup on our road.

I backed my truck up to a bin and climbed into the bed to get the computer. I could have lifted the pieces out from the ground, but it was my intention to throw the computer into the bin from the greatest height possible. Then I noticed that the next bin down was almost empty and had a large clear spot on the floor of it, which would make for a good smash when the computer hit. So I got out of the truck bed and back in the cab and pulled up alongside the next bin. These were twenty-five-foot garbage bins that were hauled in and out on tractor-trailers.

There was an attendant, a man employed by Washington County to police the dumping. When I saw him start my way I got mad, because I had a history with this man. Once he had refused to let me throw out some concrete reinforcing wire there. I ended up making it into tomato cages, which was more trouble than it was worth. Anyway, he came over with his long mop handle that he always carried and poked it into the back of my truck and said, "What's the matter with that?"

"It's old," I said.

"Don't it work?"

"I don't know. It hasn't been plugged in in two years." I was standing in the bed of my truck again, and I lifted the computer, which as I said had a metal case and was rather heavy, over my head as though I was Mighty Joe Young.

"Wait, wait, wait," the attendant said, and he rapped with his mop handle on the top of the bed wall of my truck.

I said, "Watch my truck, will you, bud?"

He stepped back and looked at my truck, which was a white Toyota and more or less beat all to hell. It was a work truck. He said, "Reckon I scratched the paint?"

I set the computer down and said, "Look, it's my truck." My face got hot.

He tilted his head at the computer and said, "Tell me, how could a man know if that thing works?"

"First he'd have to give a damn," I said. "But I don't, and this is my computer, and so therefore I'm going to smash it right now."

"No, you're not," he said. "I'll take it, and I'll see can I get some use out of it." He leaned into the back of the truck, picked up the keyboard, and turned it over.

I said, "I pay property taxes in this county."

"Help me carry this over to the office, please," he said. "I'm afraid I might drop it."

It was a pretty day out. It was sunny, but not too sunny— some white fluffy clouds were moving briskly so that the sun got broken up now and then. Even a miserable mood can be partly dispelled if the weather is pleasant. This is frustrating, because sometimes a person doesn't want his bad mood to go away. Past the five-foot chain-link fence that enclosed the dump, I noticed two silver guinea fowl standing in some high grass, looking. Their heads were light blue.

I sat down on the wall of the truck bed to have a few breaths. The man asked me where the cables were at for the computer, and I told him they were at my house in a shoe box. He would need to have them from me, he said, and also any software that went with the computer. I told him that was going to be a problem, because I would not be going back to my house for a while.

He said, "That's all right, bring them when you come by tomorrow."

"I'm not coming by tomorrow," I said. "I've temporarily left my wife. I'm not going back to the house."

He looked up into my eyes now, I guess for the first time since he'd walked over. His eyes were smudgy and didn't quite point the same direction. He said, "What's the address?"

It's strange that I got so hot about this man not letting me smash the computer, since the whole reason I had kept it in the floor at the house for two years was that I was reluctant to throw out something that had once been expensive and might conceivably still be useful to someone somewhere. This would be an example of my own stupidity. At any rate, I did not tell him the address to our house, but I did climb down from the bed and carry the computer across the gravel to his office, which was a small trailer on blocks by the fence, containing a recliner, a desk, a swag lamp, and a refrigerator. I set the computer on the desk where he told me to, and then when we were back outside in the sun he said, "If you want to smash something, smash some of them aluminum cans."

He had a barrel of cans that he had picked out of the garbage. We walked over and he tipped the barrel and shook some cans out onto the gravel. I started to jump on one of them and he said, "Hold it, fellow," and set a few of them upright in a row on a pad of smooth concrete. Then he backed up and said, "Now."

I mashed them flat one at a time. There was moderate satisfaction in it. It wasn't the same as smashing something that isn't meant to be smashed. After twenty-five or thirty cans, my foot began to hurt in the arch, and I quit. We put the flat cans into another barrel and I took my leave.

3

PROBABLY I WOULD NOT HAVE BEEN surprised by Mary's announcement that morning if I had been paying better attention to what was going on in my life. In retrospect, I can describe a couple of good reasons she had for wanting to be done with me.

First, I have already mentioned that we were remodeling. The problem was that this project had been started some time back, when we bought the house, and had dragged on ever since then so that the house was always partly torn up and unfinished.

It was an old two-story frame house in Gray, which is an unincorporated community in Washington County. The house sat on limestone blocks and had white clapboard siding, and there was a front porch that ran the length of it. There were two front doors. The windows were few and small, I suppose because the house was built by farmers who, when they wanted to see outside, just went out. I could only speculate on the need for two front doors. Like a lot of people, Mary and I had lived in rental houses and got sick of that, and wanted our own house, but never had the money. But then we saved up a little money and found this shabby place for sale by the owner, a widow named Mrs. Ott, who when we talked to her said that she had never liked living there because the house was cold and you had to have extension cords in every room, and her son was always hitting his head in the doorways, and the water ran orange after a storm, and the neighbors were idiots and had poisoned her dogs—and Mary and I fell for the place. It was on a one-lane paved road, built right up almost beside the pavement, and it came with a couple of acres including some pasture grown up with stickers and young locust trees, and a piece of creek with tall sycamores on the banks. We did not deliberate long, but then we had difficulties getting financing and insurance because of the condition of the house and its lack of central heating. There was only a wood-and-coal stove. But anything can be financed, I found out, if you are willing to pay a high enough interest rate.

So then we were in the house. The Crumleys, our nearest neighbors, were not as bad as Mrs. Ott had indicated. Certainly they were not outgoing people. They drove fast up and down the road in their trucks with their rattletrap stock trailers and made more traffic than what one would expect out of a single-family residence, but then they had cousins, and the family put out tobacco and grew hay and so on. We did not meet them for weeks, until one day one of their cows was in the road, and I walked up to their place to tell somebody. I met the lady of the house, and she thanked me and said how glad they were that Mrs. Ott had moved on.

We learned after settling in and giving things a very close look that the house indeed needed a good deal of work done to it. Every problem was more complex than it appeared. For example, you couldn't simply paint a wall, because first some trim had to be repaired. Removing the trim you would find some water damage to the drywall along the floor, and then removing the drywall you would find the skeleton of some prehistoric kind of bat, which had to be taken out with tongs, and so forth. Also, the wiring not only was antiquated but had never been up to code, even when it was installed circa the 1950s. I tore out and replaced all of it, using commercial-grade switches and receptacles, and in some places thinwall conduit. All of this was costing money, so I kept working as much as possible trying to sock something away, and Mary also worked full-time. The renovations did not proceed as quickly as we had been telling each other they would.

It wore on Mary, and I can see why. She worked hard in her low-paying job at the public library, and she deserved to come home to a decent house. Add to this the problem of heating. The woodstove did an adequate job in the living room, where it was located, but there were five rooms downstairs and two upstairs, and the house was drafty. A heat pump would have changed the whole situation, because many things can be put up with better when you're warm. Washing dishes is an example. There is nothing like being thirty-two years old and washing the dishes in a torn-up ski jacket to make you feel that life has passed you by. And then you look at the floor and there is some exposed plumbing; and then you go into the other room and there is a hole in the wallboard and some yellow fiberglass insulation sticking out where the cat pulled it; and then you go upstairs and there is your husband sitting in the floor wrapped in a quilt, rewiring some stupid antique light fixture from a flea market and watching a show about sex on the Learning Channel.

And then, another thing that didn't help was my losing a good job remodeling a house for the Paul and Paige Fleenor family of Johnson City.

It was a giant three-story house, and it was only five years old and did not need remodeling, but Mrs. Fleenor wanted to "update" the bathroom and kitchen and so on. I call her Mrs. Fleenor even though she was somewhat younger than me—I addressed her as Paige one morning when her husband was not there, and after that I noticed he began referring to her as Mrs. Fleenor whenever he spoke to me. In fact, I suspected that sometimes the only reason he spoke to me was in order to refer to his wife as Mrs. Fleenor.

It was easy money, even though by training I am an electrician and not a remodeler of houses. I can update a five-year-old bathroom about as painlessly as the next person. It doesn't require a genius, although there is such a thing as doing it the wrong way. Still, the Fleenors found problems. I would do some work and they would have me take the work out and put it back slightly different. I shouldn't have minded it, because it was all done on the clock, but I did mind it. And then what disturbed me more was when Mr. Fleenor would come home in the afternoon from his job at the TV station and inspect the day's effort and say, "You are doing good work there, Donald." Nobody calls me Donald, but unfortunately I was too proud to explain this to Mr. Fleenor, so I kept quiet and let it get under my skin, and it caused me to gradually think less highly of everyone involved.

This was a mistake. When possible, it's good to take your work seriously and to have some respect for yourself as the person who is doing the work. I don't mean to overinflate my importance, but it is true that a person who remodels another person's house is remembered for a long time. He'll be praised as the most trustworthy, hardworking salt of the earth, or he'll be spoken badly of. What I should have done was, first off, to explain that my name was Don, and second, I should have had some intelligent conversations with the Fleenors in which we figured out ways to get things done right the first time so I would not have to be pulling everything out and redoing it multiple times.

They were not bad people. But here's how I lost the job. I was on my way to the Fleenors' house in Johnson City one morning and I stopped to get some gas. While filling up I noticed the ice chest in the back of my truck and remembered that it had a beer in it, and I decided that I ought not to show up with a beer in the cooler because I knew that the Fleenors were very protemperance. What should I do with the beer, though? Throw it in the trash? I decided I needed to drink it.

I couldn't be seen drinking beer while driving my truck to work at seven-thirty in the morning, though, so I went inside the Exxon store to get a cup. The Styrofoam cups in the Exxon were the same price whether you bought a drink in them or not, and that was stupid, so I bought an enormous Exxon travel mug made of plastic which held thirty-two ounces and had a red lid. I went back out to my ice chest and it turned out there were two beers there, not one. I poured one into the mug and it looked pitiful, like hardly anything, so I put the other one in and it still looked like not very much. I placed the empty bottles in the trash and drove to Johnson City the long way up 36, enjoying my two pretty cold Natural Lights.

Usually two beers don't mean a whole lot to me, but I guess I'd had a light breakfast. I was about to the Fleenors' house and I thought, Look at me, I shouldn't show up this way. I'm impaired. I should call in sick. And then I thought, That Mr. Fleenor is a jerk. And then I thought, Hey I'm pretty good. Me impaired is every bit as good as the next man at the height of his powers. So I decided to go on and show up.

I was feeling friendly when I got there. I was talkative. Mrs.

Fleenor seemed to notice this and enjoy it. I asked her to come into the bathroom so I could show her what I was doing and we could have a conversation about what kind of corner to use in the shower tile. She came in and was talking and cheerful, and I was standing in the shower stall yakking on and I pointed at something, and she bent in to look, and then suddenly she stood up straight and stared at me, and then she turned and left the bathroom.

At lunch that day Mr. Fleenor came home. He took me out on the deck and we had a talk. He said, "Mrs. Fleenor says that she smelled a beer on your breath this morning. Is that true, Donald?"

"No, it isn't," I said. "In reality, Mrs. Fleenor smelled two beers on my breath."

It was a grave day in the Fleenor household. Heads hung low. Everyone was disappointed.

Even I was disappointed. The Fleenors got very moralistic and told me to leave. I left, and then I proceeded to make the worst of things. Instead of calling up any number of people who had asked me to do work lately—I could have gotten work that same day—I drove back to the Exxon where my mug came from and I bought a cold twelve-pack. I wasn't depressed or thirsty exactly but I could sense both of those feelings coming on, and I wanted to head them off. If nothing else it would have been better for me to go home and go to bed, but instead I took the twelve-pack to Boone Lake Dam and sat in my truck and drank all but one. I left this last one on a concrete picnic table for someone else to find.

Now that I look back at that whole episode it seems as though I was looking for a reason to get drunk, and lacking one, made one. I got myself fired.

It was wrong. It wasn't evil, I don't believe, but unwise and impractical. If it was evil at all, it was only evil towards myself, and I guess towards Mary, which makes it evil through and through.

Why drink? It is fun. I like it, or as I heard a man say the other day about his Corvair that he had restored, "We like enjoying it." Really I would say there are two kinds of drinking, and one is for fun, and the other is preemptive of nonfun. When you drink out of boredom, restlessness, habit, or the feeling that you are soon going to be depressed, that is the preemptive kind.

What is "depressed"? Medically, I believe, it has to do with the heartbeat getting fainter and the eyes less bright. The reason I think this is that once we had a kitten who'd been bit by a dog, and we took him to the vet and the vet wrote on the paper that the kitten was suffering from "systemic depression" as a result of his skull being cracked. The kitten was in bad shape, but he got better. But in the nonmedical sense depression means, for me anyway, having the feeling that something you deserve has been taken away from you.

Well, not always. Sometimes you get that feeling and it just makes you angry, for example when the county-dump man wouldn't let me smash my computer. Anger is when you feel you have been robbed and you mean to do something about it. Depression is when you feel you've been robbed and you either can't do anything about it or don't have the energy to do anything about it. That's what it means to be depressed.

Beer for depressed people is a way of inducing forgetfulness, dissolving the knot, and even of taking a bit of revenge on yourself for being lazy. It is a way of both babying and punishing yourself at the same time. What power there is in this useful tool of beer. That must account for its long-standing popularity among all walks of people, all of whom are subject to feelings of depression, or the sense of having been permanently robbed of their due happiness.

And so, where was I? Things that didn't help. It didn't help when I came home drunk as a finch before dark on a Wednesday and told Mary from the stairs that I was going straight to bed because I didn't feel well, and by the way I also got fired from my good job with the Fleenors for not feeling well. She didn't lay into me then—it was a quiet time, as I remember it. I was lying on the bed upstairs and I said, "I'm getting worse," and she asked me what was wrong with me—the lights were off and it was kind of blue and shady and quiet upstairs, and she sat on a chair not far from the bed—and I told her I'd had too much to drink. And then I told her Paul Fleenor had told me not to come back, and why, and then I may have gone to sleep because I remember later sitting up and thinking that Mary had left, but she was there and had the lamp on— whether she'd left and come back or been sitting there the whole time, I didn't know. And I had no idea whether she was really mad, like butcher-knife mad, or feeling sorry for me and nice, or maybe feeling bored and only waiting around for something to happen. I reached over and found her knee. And then I remember thinking, I believe she is unhappy, but I'm too screwed up to tell.

4.

THAT I COULD HAVE THE GOOD LUCK to be married to
Mary and still consider myself deprived of my due happiness
was a sign of something wrong with me, I think. Something
needed adjustment.

Let's go back to the Saturday afternoon when I had just run
off from the house and gone by the dump. Of course, this was
not the happiest time for me, in fact I was miserable, yet there
was a feeling about the afternoon that was lively and not
unpleasant. It's perverse, but part of me was thinking, or wanting to think, I'm free! My wife had cut me loose, and what
married person can say there is not somewhere deep in the
uglier part of his soul a question mark that is wondering,
Wouldn't we be better off apart? Or rather, Wouldn't I be better off? I had the question mark. So in spite of my knowing
that I loved Mary and was now desolate, a part of me couldn't
help thinking, This is a damned boon. I am out here, world.

To celebrate and to promote this upbeat view of events, I
stopped at an Exxon and bought a Slim Jim and one of these
handy packages of six bottles of beer that comes in its own
cardboard carrying case. They are widely available. I also got a

bag of ice and I placed it along with the six beers into the ice chest that happened conveniently to be sitting in the back of my truck where it always is. I then opened my Slim Jim and began eating it but did not open a beer. I drove my truck and went riding, looking at the day. It was June. I drove into Johnson City and went to Kroger, and I had no particular purpose for being there except that I had noticed several times before when I had been inside this Kroger that it seemed to be full of beautiful and interesting women. The prices on the food were somewhat elevated. I stopped there and took a walk through, and there were one or two interesting-looking ladies, but to see them made me feel like a piece of old disgusting rug.

I was only browsing, anyway—I did not have anything more than that in mind. I bought a loaf of Roman Meal bread and left.

Depression was on its way, then. I could tell—it was like the smell of ozone, the famous rain-is-coming smell. I was planning a drunk but I needed a place to have it in, because I wanted to be smart about it and not drink and drive a lot, and I don't go in much for drinking in bars. Should I check in to a motel somewhere, I wondered? Well, if so why not just go buy myself a nice piece of scratchy rope and put a noose in it, because it would seem about equally cheerful.

I drove back through Boone's Creek towards Gray, and then on out 75 towards Sulphur Springs. I drove to my friend Ken McInturff's place. He is a gentleman about twenty years my senior, and I'd worked with him a number of times and had a number of beers with him after work. We were not in the habit of dropping by each other's homes unannounced, but my hope was that I would drive by and spot him in a lawn chair outside his shop drinking beer, and then I could pull over to visit as though I'd happened by.

When I got there he was on his new Gravely zero-turn-radius mower, whirling it over the lawn. I started to keep going on past, but my truck is recognizable enough that he spotted me. It used to say BRUSH ELECTRICAL on the doors, but the truck is such a beater that McInturff told me it was bad advertising, so I painted the sign out with red primer. Now there were dull red blotches on the doors.

"Come the hell over and have a beer," he said. "Sit down while I finish mowing." He pointed to a stack of plastic chairs after placing in my hand a cold bottle, which he had taken from the refrigerator in his shop. I took a chair and did as I was told, and have hardly ever been more grateful to anyone for telling me what to do. It was a great relief. The shop was cool and shady, and full of old tractors, which McInturff rebuilt. There also was his pickup, a '96 GMC with maybe twelve thousand miles on it, a rolling shrine. The more I noticed how relieved I was to be there, sheltered as it were by friendship, the more I almost feared that old McInturff might come back to the shop and find me sniffling.

I drank the beer and got up to get the six-pack out of my truck and put it in his refrigerator. McInturff gave me a thumbs-up from his Gravely. In a little bit he had finished and he rode the mower into the shop.

The Gravely was red, and the mowing deck was mounted on the front. In place of a steering wheel it had two levers. By working these in opposite directions, the operator could cause the mower to spin in place. It was a nice piece of equipment, and McInturff was proud of it, so when he shut it off inside the shop I asked him wasn't he going to hose the thing off before putting it away.

"Not while I have company," he said.

"Quit being nice," I said.

He opened himself a beer, using the bib from his overalls to twist the cap off.

"You like to wash your Gravely in the nude," I said.

He sat down and removed his hat in order to wipe down his head with a towel. His hair was red, like his mower. We talked about what he had done all morning. He'd had a calf die, so he and a neighbor had taken it to Iris Glen, the landfill in Johnson City, which was the only landfill that would accept dead livestock. I told him I had figured he was busy but I'd been driving by and thought I'd stop, and so on. He said with gravity that he had set aside this afternoon for the special purpose of drinking several cold Natural Light beers.

I asked him about his tractors, which was a known way to get him talking indefinitely. He had lately found something for his 1938 "styled" John Deere A, a certain kind of knob or something, I forget exactly what, but it was something important. We went to the A and he started it up and let it run awhile where it sat, and we listened with some pleasure. It was loud and steady, with the putt-putt rhythm that I'm told is characteristic of the big two-cylinder engines.

Then Dove Ellender arrived, hollering something about the qualifyings. It was three or four in the afternoon. McInturff shut the A off, and Dove started hollering at me.

"Wendell!" he yelled in his enormous deep and booming voice. Wendell is what I was sometimes called in this circle, because of somebody named Wendell that someone had known sometime whom I reminded them of because I had once cleaned out the gutter on the top of a beer can with my shirttail before opening it.

Dove yelled, "McInturff, we need to watch the damn qualifyings!"

McInturff said, "If that's what we must do, I don't think Grace will object." Grace was his wife.

I skulled my beer. When McInturff saw me turn my bottle up he jumped to the refrigerator and handed me a new one.

"Come help me lift this damn television out of my truck," Dove said.

McInturff and I went out onto the freshly cut grass where Dove had parked his truck, and we saw the television in back.

"I thought we'd watch the qualifyings in your shop, McInturff," Dove said. "I knowed you'd be out here drinking."

I lowered the tailgate, set my beer on the ground, and lifted the television out. I carried it into the shop and set it on a tool bench, then went back outside to retrieve my beer. McInturff cleared a receptacle and meanwhile, Dove was getting into a chair. He was somewhat older than McInturff and was not in good health, and he didn't walk well. Sometimes it was troubling to watch him, because he'd stumble and have to grab something. Most times he only had one hand to grab with, because the other was holding a foam-rubber bottle holder with a bottle of beer in it. He was a tall and big-handed man with, as I've said, an enormous voice, in spite of having smoked like a fish for eight tenths of his life. He was a formidable presence in his way.

"Wendell, how are you, buddy?" Dove said.

"I'm doing all right," I said. "It's nice out here, isn't it?" McInturff's shop had a large sliding metal door and we sat just inside, with the door wide open.

"It is a damn beautiful day," Dove said, and he uncapped his bottle using a bottle capper from his pocket. McInturff set a hubcap on the concrete beside Dove and said it was an ashtray, and Dove thanked him and dropped the bottle cap in.

McInturff sat down and asked Dove, "Did you bring the remote?"

"No, I left it at the house."

"Will you drive to the house then and turn the TV on to the qualifyings, please?"

"Why didn't you turn it on when you was at the set just now?" Dove said.

I started to feel a little buzz.

McInturff got up and turned on the television. The picture was snow. He turned the volume up all the way and shouted over the static, "What channel are the qualifyings on?"

Dove bolted up very straight in his chair, then started bouncing from side to side quickly. "TNN!" he said.

"That's channel 204," McInturff said, and he bent over to punch it in on the buttons at the base of the television.

"It's on cable!" Dove said. He called out a series of profanities. "You knew that, you son of a bitch."

McInturff looked at me dumbly.

"Turn off the damn television!" Dove said.

"If you knew it's on cable, why did you bring the television set over here?" McInturff said.

"I forgot!"

McInturff turned off the television and sat down with us. We were quiet for a moment. Then McInturff said, "I guess we could go in the house and watch the damn qualifyings."

"Nope, I can't smoke in the house," Dove said, and he was lighting a cigarette as he said it.

"It's true, Grace wouldn't appreciate that," McInturff said.

They talked awhile about someone I didn't know. I sat holding my beer and feeling, in a provisional way, contented. McInturff said of somebody, "I'd as soon shoot him as back over him." He and Dove had been friends for decades, and anytime

I was around them, I didn't know who they were talking about most of the time.

McInturff said, "Shall we turn on the television again and see if the reception is any better?"

Dove said, "Let's not."

Dove went on about this person they'd been talking about, whose name was Jimbo. "Well he's back, and she says he's staying," Dove said.

"Has he got a job?"

"She claims he's selling cars. She's quit her job and says he's going to support them all while she stays at home. I'm so damn mad about it I can't see straight."

"You can't walk straight, so why would you need to see straight?" McInturff said.

Dove frowned at me. "Why don't she see through that bullshit?" he said. "I don't want to talk about it."

"I can tell you don't," McInturff said.

"If I was ten years younger and in better health, I'd personally knock the crap out of that weasel. Because he's stupid, and he's worthless. I was no model parent, Wendell, but at least I had the sense to stay gone once I run off. Damn."

Then Dove straightened up and burped, and then he said, "I'm going to leave this television here in your shop awhile, McInturff. It's too heavy for me to carry it home today."

"Who put it in the car?"

"Junie."

"Now I understand," McInturff said. "This whole adventure was a ploy to make Junie bend over."

"Yes, and she did bend over too," Dove said. He turned to me and said, "Junie likes to lay out topless in the yard sometimes, Wendell. I can set a chair right beside her in the grass, and she don't mind it."

"She knows you're not a threat," McInturff said.

"That's the sad truth," Dove said. "I ain't been a threat to nobody for some time."

"You're a threat to yourself," McInturff said.

"Well, maybe."

I got up and got each of us another beer.

"I don't know if I'm even a threat to myself anymore," Dove said.

"Give yourself some credit," McInturff said. "A man like you could whip the living shit out of a man like you."

"Kiss my ass."

"Not with Wendell here."

"Shut up, asshole." Dove got up out of his chair with much trouble and announced he was going out the back door to use the facilities. He moved off slowly, touching things as he walked to steady himself. McInturff got up and hid Dove's beer behind a tool cabinet. A car horn honked out front and McInturff's arm shot up in the air. Someone was driving by, waving.

Dove returned, looked at the spot on the floor where his beer had been, and got another beer out of the refrigerator. He and McInturff got to talking about Dove's wild fighting days back in his youth. "I was staying at that rock house of Grover's in Bluff City," Dove said. "I had the day off, so I was trying to sleep. I didn't never get a day off then. Well, some asshole was beating on the door. I ignored it and went back to sleep, but the asshole wouldn't stop. So I got up and swung the door open, and there's Atteberry with a linoleum knife back over his head like this"—Dove showed us with his arm—"and then he brung it down and I shut the door, and he busted his damn hand open. Well, I didn't feel like fooling with him. Then he started rapping on windows, and I went in the kitchen and started some coffee, let it drip, and drank a cup. Then I stepped out the back door and around to the front, and there Atteberry was, trying to work his linoleum knife out of the door frame, and he had cut his finger almost off. That poor idiot. I stepped up beside him and knocked him the hell down, and then I grabbed him and locked him in his own damn trunk of his car."

"Bullshit," I said.

"Oh, it's true," Dove said. "Blood was on the porch ceiling." McInturff nodded at me.

"Then I drove his car to his mother's house, him in the trunk of it."

"What was he mad about?"

"Same thing all of us are," McInturff said.

"I may have kissed his girlfriend," Dove said.

"Then she turned into a toad," McInturff said, "which is what pissed off Wes Atteberry."

"Atteberry was a bit of a dumbass," Dove said.

"Yes he was," McInturff said.

"His daddy was a nice one, though."

"His daddy was as nice as they come."

"Hell yes he was!" Dove said. He stubbed out a cigarette and took a baby sip from his beer and then said, "By the way, asshole, I know you hid my beer."

McInturff turned to me and said, "Did you ever know a man who would sit and hold a conversation with his own rectum?"

"When it starts talking back, I'd worry," I said.

McInturff laughed.

We passed the time, and then Dove said he was going home to go to bed. McInturff turned to me rather suddenly and blinked and said, "Grace and I are going out to supper tonight, Don, if you and Mary would like to join us."

I was a slight bit drunk, and I found myself pretending to be drunker than I was. I said slowly, "Well, thank you, McInturff. I guess we had better stay home." I didn't mean to be lying, but I did lie. "I think Mary's planned something for supper tonight."

"Okay," McInturff said.

I stood up. I said something hokey-sounding to the effect that it had been good seeing them both. Maybe everyone has these moments when you feel like you are about to fall open, and anything you say might come out wrong and sound too emotional, or something. Well, so I shut up and left.

5

THEN I GOT THE IDEA that if I did go home and eat supper, I would not have lied.

I arrived home at six-thirty P.M. to find Mary not there. I walked up the stairs, full of dread, to see whether she had taken her bag, and I was relieved to find it still open and unpacked on the bed. I looked for a note or some indication of where she might be and did not find any. The dog was lying in the floor in the living room, and he watched me check the answering machine. No word.

The cat was yowling at my ankles, which meant that it hadn't been fed. That told me Mary would be coming back tonight, one way or another. She would not leave the animals without food.

On the other hand, if she came home and spotted my truck in the driveway, she would know I had fed the animals and she might keep on going. I couldn't risk that, because what I wanted above all else was for Mary to stay in the house. That meant I had to leave.

I fed the dog and cat and quickly made myself a sandwich. I put the rest of the Roman Meal loaf in the refrigerator, and while I was there, I grabbed an armful of beers. I went back to my truck and drove down our road, across the little bridge over the creek, and onto the gravel drive to our neighbor George Massey's farm. I had to stop and open a gap in a fence, pull my truck through, and close the gap behind me. Then I drove uphill through George Massey's cow pasture to his barn, which was on top of a ridge that overlooked our house. There I stayed, eating my sandwich and drinking my beers and watching for my wife to come home.

It turned dark. It was approximately nine-thirty when she pulled up our road and into the driveway. Her headlights went off, and I heard the car door slam, and then a long time went by. Then she was in the house switching on lights. Twenty minutes later the lights in our shabby-looking house went out.

I had been standing in the bed of my truck to see better. Now I went to climb down. Dew had gathered on the surface of the truck and my shoe slipped, and I took a hard spill into the damp grass. I picked myself up and shut myself into the cab.

I imagined Mary by herself down there in our bed, maybe crying, and I thought I was a bastard and ought to go to her and just say anything, whatever I could think of to make things better. Was it possible? Was there anything to say? Was there perhaps a way, if I could not make things really better, to make them seem better?

Then I imagined going down to the house and in and up the stairs and finding her curled up with the dog on the sofa, eating popcorn and watching a movie, very contented. If that was the true picture, I didn't want to see it. I wanted her to be at least as torn up as I was.

I considered the problem from many angles and somehow finally went to sleep. I was awakened unpleasantly by the sensation that someone was knocking on the side of my head. In fact, it was George Massey, the owner of the pasture, thumping on the window glass of my truck. I twisted around to see him and rubbed my eyes. I had forgotten where I was.

He motioned for me to roll my window down. I did it, and he stuck his head almost inside the truck. "What's going on up here?" he said.

It was daylight. George's white hair gleamed in the early sun, and the end of his small nose was nearly poking my cheek. I opened my door slightly to ease him away from me. "I fell asleep," I said.

"You fell asleep? Well—" He backed away several steps and looked at the ground, and then up at me. "You say you fell asleep up here?"

I'll skip over a bit of what followed, but basically it involved me repeating another nine times that yes, I had fallen asleep in my truck in his cow pasture. George was at that time eighty years old, and I wonder if he always needed things repeated or if it was a trait he developed. At any rate, once we had established that yes, I had been spying on my house and no, I did not want to talk about it, he was kind enough to change the subject. He asked me if I had a minute to help him reset his mailbox. Someone had pulled it out of the ground the night before, he said.

Well, sure I would help, I said.

"Have you got my posthole diggers?"

"Yes, they're in the barn across from the house, George." He had lent them to me.

"We'll need those," he said.

I said, "It's difficult for me to go back to the house right now. That's why I'm up here, see."

He squinted at me and scratched the back of his hand. He sighed and leaned back against the side of his truck, which he had driven up to the barn like I had. "We have to clean the hole out before we can put the post back in," he said.

We got in our trucks and I followed him to his house. After trying a couple of methods, I finally lay down on my stomach and cleaned out the hole with my hand. Then I climbed down the creek bank and retrieved his mailbox from where the vandals had flung it. It was still securely on its post. We lowered it back into the hole and tamped it in place with two shovel handles. Then I knocked some of the dirt off myself and told George I needed to run along.

"Everyone's in a hurry," he said.

I left. It was Sunday morning. I drove past the Primitive Baptist Church at the corner of Douglas Shed Road a mile from our house, and cars were parked on the grass and all along the side of the road. I did not feel fresh, owing to the dirty job I had helped George with, and even more, sleeping in my truck. Sleeping in any kind of vehicle overnight is a great way to make yourself feel slimy and unappealing.

In my wallet I had seven dollars, so I went to the Sit-N-Bull Restaurant in downtown Gray and washed up some and then got some coffee and a late breakfast. The waitress, whose name was Ellen, spilled half a cup of coffee in my lap and either didn't see it or chose to pretend it hadn't happened. I also chose to pretend it hadn't happened.

I ate my breakfast. I had noticed at the next table a woman in a gold fabric shirt with a big man, and it seemed she was looking at me. Midway through my breakfast, the woman leaned over towards me and said, "I am very impressed that you haven't said a word about the coffee the waitress spilled on you. You're a real gentleman."

The man she was with was staring straight ahead and didn't look at me.

"It wasn't that hot," I said.

The big man said, "She'll be back to warm it up."

Outside of the restaurant there was a pay phone. I stood by my truck in the parking lot, looking at the phone and thinking, Should I call her? No, I shouldn't. Then I thought about my folks, who lived in Knoxville. My mother called every Sunday evening without fail unless I called her first. She'd be calling tonight, and what would Mary tell her? I decided to call my folks.

They weren't home. I tried my mother's cell phone and got her voice mail and left a message saying "Hey Mom, it's Don, I was just calling to say hi and so you wouldn't have to call back tonight, so don't call back, I love you, bye," and I hung up. Well, that was obviously no good, so I called back and said, "Mom, the reason I don't want you to call back is that Mary and I are going out tonight to a movie and a party, so I just wanted to let you know, but I'll talk to you soon, bye." Again I had lied without meaning to.

6

THEN I STARTED THINKING about my mom and dad's age, and their death, which would sooner or later take place. I sat in my truck in the parking lot outside Sit-N-Bull and little spasms of mourning passed over me, even though my folks were not so old—middle sixties—and were having a fun life, I thought, retired early, traveling often and seeing their friends and working in the yard and all of that. It wasn't their age but the fact of their mortality that was occurring to me. And then it occurred to me that I too was also mortal, and the reality of that hit me, and the reality of Mary's mortality—and I thought of something from the previous morning that I haven't mentioned. At one point after she had been packing clothes, I looked at her and there were faint bags under her eyes—faint soft-looking places—and she looked for a moment older than I had ever seen her look. I'm not saying she wasn't beautiful, because she was. But this minute sign of her aging and of time passing came back to me now in my truck like a blow to the chest, so to speak. I thought, What do we have ahead of us, fifty more years of life? For the first time I can remember ever doing so, I pictured that. I thought back over the past year, and things that had happened—a new foot valve on the well pump, a dime-an-hour raise for Mary—and stuff that had happened outdoors, like winter and spring, the leaves and weather—and I thought okay, that is one year of life. Times it by fifty, and that's what is left. And then I loved Mary, and I wanted to go home to her.

But instead I went back to the pay phone and called her. I got the answering machine, and I left a message saying that it was very hard to stay away, but I was doing it because I knew she wanted me to. Then I felt like a jerk and I hung up.

And then, a person can only ponder death and be miserable about it for so long, so I began to consider my truck, and I got the idea that it would be a good thing to do to paint it. For one thing, as I have already indicated, it needed painting. For another thing, it would demonstrate to Mary, possibly, that I was going to turn a new leaf. I drove, right that moment, to Walter Furlong's body shop in Kingsport on the off chance that he might be there on a Sunday morning, and sure enough, he was. The bay door was raised five feet and he was sitting outside it on a five-gallon driveway-sealer can. Who else should be there as well but Dove Ellender. "Wendell!" Dove said.

"Hello, Dove," I said. "Hello, Walter."

Walter pulled a Natural Light bottle out from behind his sealer can, where he must have hid it when he saw someone was driving up. It was not yet time for church to be out, and some people are old-fashioned about when it is right to have a beer. Dove on the other hand had not bothered to hide his.

"Pull up some furniture," Walter said. "You want a beer?"

I said it was a bit early for me.

"I'm just finishing one up from last night," Walter said.

Walter, who is missing one ear, asked me what I knew good. We conversed a bit, and then I told him I needed my truck painted. This made him frown, because he was something of a perfectionist and the truck needed bodywork. He said he generally would not paint something that was full of dents.

"How much to fix the dents?" I asked him.

"Twenty-five thousand dollars."

I told him I needed to have the truck painted for my wife, as a token of the overall improvement that she could be expecting out of me.

He asked Dove if that didn't sound like an example of the worst possible bullshit ever. Yes, Dove said, it did.

"I need it painted today," I said.

"Today is Sunday," Walter said.

I said, "You'll drink on Sunday, but you won't paint my truck in order to save my marriage?"

"I'll paint it right now, for a hundred dollars, metallic reef. Is it clean?"

"I'll go drive it through a car wash," I said.

"That's not good enough," he said. "You'll have to wash it yourself right now, where it sits."

"Have you got some soap?"

He told me where it was. I washed the truck while they watched me, smoking cigarettes. Then I dried it, then they moved their seats and Walter raised the bay door, and I pulled the truck into the bay. Walter said, "You're paying cash, right?"

"Don't you take credit cards?"

He shook his head, but he went on and started taping the trim anyway.

I sat down with Dove and we watched. He said, "What in the hell is this about you and Mary?"

I explained that she had announced she was moving out but that I had left first, meaning she had to stay in the house.

"She don't have to stay if she don't want to," Dove said.

"Yes she does, to feed the dog and cat," I said.

He took a moment to process that, and then he said, "I'm not sure it works that way, Wendell."

I asked him what he had been up to.

"I was trying to get some help moving some furniture."

"I can help you," I said. "Where are you moving it to?"

"Mississippi."

I asked him what was in Mississippi.

"My daughter Rhonda," he said. He lit a cigarette that was in his lips. Walter, who was doing something to the air compressor, said, "Shit on it!" We looked back in there, but he seemed okay. Dove stood up carefully and pulled out his billfold and looked inside it, then sat down again on his chair and carefully, with the ends of his fingers, extracted a picture of a woman who looked about my age. It was a portrait studio shot, and the woman in the picture was astonishingly good-looking. I said, "Is this your daughter?"

"That's Rhonda," he said. "Hard to believe, isn't it?"

"Yes." Dove was such a big and coarse specimen of a man that it was surprising to find anything so attractive having sprung from him.

"And that's her boy Michael," he said. He showed me a picture of a child in a diaper—another studio portrait—and the child was standing in a galvanized metal tub on Astroturf with some packages of soap lying around. The child was one to three years old, and there wasn't much that was distinct about him to notice.

When I held the picture out to give it back, Dove was staring off past my shoulder, and his face had changed. I looked away, because I thought he was about to cry, but then to my relief he sneezed. He put the pictures away.

I gave in and got into the beer with them. Soon Walter was

ready to spray. What came out on the door of my truck was a kind of turquoise color that had metal flakes in it. It was ugly. Dove looked at me, then busted out laughing.

I said, "That's fine. I like it."

"You better like it!" Dove said. "Because it's on there!"

Walter set the spray gun down on the concrete, pulled his mask down so it covered his throat, and stepped over to where we were sitting. He watched me and didn't say anything. I looked at him, and then I looked at Dove, and nobody spoke, and Walter got a beer from the orange ice chest in the corner, and then he went back to spraying. Dove thumped my arm and laughed again.

We watched the paint go on. It was horrible. It looked like a Popsicle color. I wanted to like it, though, because a hundred dollars is a chunk of money, to me, anyway. I worked on it, and by the time Walter was finished and asked me, "What's the verdict?" I was able to say with conviction, "That's a fine-looking paint job, Walter. I'm proud."

Dove said, "It looks like a damn circus wagon."

"They use that paint on bicycles," Walter said.

"Well, I like it."

Dove said, "Bullshit! You hate it, Wendell!"

I did, but I was determined to like it. I said, "Wonder what color I ought to paint my logo on there."

Dove said, "You ain't got no logo."

"The hell I don't," I said, and I pulled out my wallet and took out and showed him my business card. It said BRUSH ELECTRICAL and had my home phone number on it, and at the top of the card it had a man's head wearing a cap to one side and winking with a little lightning bolt next to him.

"Why, you do so have a logo," Dove said after studying it.

He handed the card to Walter, and Walter held it at arm's length to make it out.

"I'm painting that logo on both doors," I said.

"You mean you're having it painted," Walter said.

"Okay."

"Yellow will be the most eye-catching," he said. "Like one of the NAPA trucks with the yellow hat on top."

"Them are ugly as shit," Dove said.

I reached and took my card back from Walter and put it back in my wallet.

"Is that your last one?" Walter asked.

"No."

"It is too," he said. "Better keep it." He and Dove laughed at me.

I asked him how soon I could drive my truck.

"Depending on the weather, Tuesday," Walter said.

"Not today?"

"Tuesday."

"Will you mind if I sleep in it till then?"

He said he didn't know if it would be good for his business to have me shuffling around in my shorts and slippers in his shop first thing in the morning.

"I don't wear slippers," I said.

"Do you wear shorts?"

Dove said, "If he don't, he can paint his self metallic reef and won't nobody know the difference. They'll think he's wearing blue tights."

Walter said, "I've used up the very last of the metallic reef, thank goodness."

"You can masking-tape him, then," Dove said.

"Or he can tape himself."

"If anybody here tapes me, it will damn sure be myself," I said.

A lull followed in which beers were sipped and cigarettes dragged on. Then Dove said, "So you are not welcome at the house, Wendell."

"I'm welcome, but if I go home, she'll leave."

"What in the hell did you do?"

"I don't know. A lot of things."

"What set it off, though?"

"I don't know. She got up yesterday morning and packed." Walter was looking at the pavement, I saw.

Dove said, "Well, you must have screwed up somewhere along the line, Wendell. You haven't been dallying, I hope."

"No, hell no. It's not like that," I said. "The truth is, I'm in love with my wife."

"Aw shit," Dove said, and he got up and made his way carefully back to the bathroom.

Walter and I didn't have much to say to each other. He got up and walked over to my truck and examined the paint up close. I stood up to follow but he gave me a stop signal with his hand. I went to his ice chest and got a beer. The ice had melted, and the bottles were at the bottom of the chest under four inches of cold water.

Dove came out of the bathroom and told a story about when one of his wives got so mad at him that she emptied out a sugar tin of his money on the bed and set the money on fire.

Walter said, "How much of money was in that canister, Dove?"

"Over a thousand dollars."

"Is that right?"

"I put it out by jumping on it, and me naked as the day."

"You never did quite get over that, did you?" Walter said.

"I never got over a lot of things. Thus I come to be the person I am today." Dove flicked his lighter seven times, threw it in the trash, pulled another lighter from his shirt pocket, and lit his cigarette. Then he sat down and looked at me and said in a deep voice, "This ain't good, Wendell."

I nodded.

He said, "You know what the smartest thing is that you could do right now?"

"Whatever Dove doesn't tell you," Walter said.

"The smartest thing in the world that you could do right now is to go home and ask her to forgive you," Dove said. "I do not give a shit what you done, or thought you done, or meant to did, or nothing. Just go home and say 'I'm sorry.'"

Walter held up a push broom and said, "You can take this too, honey. You'll be needing it."

I didn't completely like Walter. He was one of the boys, though.

Dove said, "Walter, you don't understand this. Wendell has a good thing, and a person ought to preserve something like that. There comes a point, and I will tell you this and it is the damn truth, when your pride does not mean nothing. Dignity, forget that. And if you don't believe me, then wait till you get my age and try to piss."

"I don't want to hear about your pissing troubles again," Walter said.

Dove turned in his chair to face Walter and said, "Why are you so sour?"

Walter ignored him.

Dove pointed his finger at me and said, "Don't go home drunk!"

"I can't go home period."

"That's right," Walter said. "His paint is wet."

"Maybe someone will give you a lift," Dove said.

It started to rain lightly. We moved our seats. It occurred to me that you do not get a good paint job, painting in wet weather.

But then I thought, Who cares?

7

WE SAT AROUND FOREVER, drinking and delaying the next move. Dove said he would like to have offered me his couch to sleep on, but it was going to hopefully be loaded into the back of his truck before bedtime. I was welcome to sleep on his floor if I could stand it.

I told him thanks but I didn't want to impose.

"Dove's is the traditional house to land in when your old lady gives you the boot," Walter said. "I was there the better part of a month when me and Noodle were getting our divorce."

"I never said I was getting a divorce," I said.

"I never said it either, but you might be."

I'd heard enough out of Walter. I stood up. "Thanks for everything," I said.

"What are you thanking me for?" he said.

"I don't know." I started over to my truck, and Walter asked me what I was doing.

"Leaving," I said.

"You can't drive that truck with wet paint on it! Don't you dare touch the truck!" he said. "Get back!" He jumped up off of his sealer can and ran at me, then stopped as though I held a gun. I reached my hand towards the truck's fender. I stepped closer to it, and he said, "Cut it out, asshole!"

"Whose truck is it?" I said.

"I've got more in the paint than you've got in the truck!"

"Okay. Well, bye then," I said, and I walked out into the drizzle without any more talk.

It was coming down lightly but steadily. I crossed to the other side of the street, where there was an awning over the sidewalk. I had gone the length of the block when Dove slowed down in his truck alongside me. He called out the passenger-side window, "Hey, get in, Wendell."

"I don't mind walking in a drizzle," I said.

"Where in the hell are you going to go?"

"I don't know, and it doesn't matter."

"Get in, and you can help me load my couch in the truck. All right?"

I got in.

Dove's truck was a 1969 half-ton Ford longbed. Bodywise, it was in not quite as good a shape as my Toyota, which is to say it was in poor shape. There was considerable rust and dentage. The paint scheme was as follows: the cab roof was white, then the truck was flat green down to the chrome strip of trim above the fenders, and then below that it was white again. Inside, the seat was covered in a woven plastic fabric, the factory upholstery, no doubt, which was fairly well intact. The dash was metal, of course, but with a cushion strip along the top to bounce your head on in a wreck. The hole where the radio belonged was empty, and a length of wire with brown insulation dangled out. The wire was labeled "radio" with a piece of masking tape. The ashtray was pulled out, and it had only bottle caps in it. Dove was of the Toss Butts Out Window school.

As he drove, a cigarette bobbled from his lips, and he scowled as though driving required some physical exertion. I asked him if the truck had power steering.

"Of course it has power steering," he said. He pulled his elbows back against his ribs like a bird and steered with one finger to show me. "I wish everything worked as well as this power steering," he said.

Dove's house was on Wilcox Drive, a bland thoroughfare that cuts between the interstate and downtown Kingsport. To one side of him was a convenience store with a half-acre parking lot and two gas pumps, and behind that was the trailer where Junie and her boyfriend lived. To the other side of Dove's yard was a steep drive leading to a concrete and gravel plant. Beyond the plant was the South Fork of the Holston River, and beyond that was the Eastman Chemical plant. Across Wilcox, facing Dove's house, was a golf course attached to the new Kingsport convention center.

We got to his house and he backed across the front yard up to the porch. In the driveway was a horse trailer. I remarked on it and he said, "Yep. We're going to load that, too."

I followed him in the front door and to the sofa in the living room. The sofa was eight feet long and upholstered in beige vinyl. "It's a Hide-a-Bed," Dove said.

I went to one end and thumped the arm. The sofa was built like a hippopotamus.

"I'll be back," Dove said, and he left out the front door.

I had visited Dove's a few times before, to sit with him and McInturff and sometimes Walter and any of a number of other friends, drinking after the workday. Dove lived here alone but held court each afternoon in the living room from this sofa. There was a coffee table in front of it that held the remote control, the portable phone, the TV listings, a dinner-plate-sized ashtray, and a cluster of prescription bottles. Dove always sat at the right arm of the sofa, the one I had thumped. There were chairs along the other walls, except for the wall that held the television cabinet and a few paperbacks and some Richard Petty memorabilia. There was also a Richard Petty clock over the sofa, and in a corner was a shadow box containing Dove's mother's collection of decorative sugar spoons. The walls and ceiling were brown from cigarette smoke, and the window glass looked like it had been shellacked. The carpet, however, was new, and it had parallel vacuum tracks in it. Anytime I'd been there, the house was tidy.

Dove came back with a kid whom I recognized as the clerk from the convenience store next door. He was a short but burly person whose legs were covered in green tattoos from the knees down, possibly above that as well. I had bought beer from him many times. Dove taped the cushions in place, and then the young man and I lifted the sofa up off the floor and carried it edgewise through the front doorway. He was as strong as a little bull, and he flipped the sofa around as though it meant nothing to him. Some people play tough in a situation like this, but I don't, and I let the kid know I was not up to that kind of exercise. I was groaning and cursing the whole time.

A customer pulled up wanting gas next door, and Tattoo Boy had to leave. Dove shook his long head slowly. "I got more to be loaded," he said.

"What else?" I said.

"All them chairs in the living room."

"That all goes to your daughter?"

"Yep. They moved to a house and ain't got furniture."

"Where will you sit when you come back?"

His eyes got big and he shrugged.

The chairs were easy after the sofa. I put them in the back of the horse trailer, which was already half loaded with boxes, and then I gave Dove hand signals while he backed the truck up to hitch the trailer on. The truck had an automatic transmission and lurched whenever he took his foot off the brake, but we managed. The plug for the trailer lights did not match the jack on the truck's bumper, and I asked Dove if he wanted me to rig something up so he would have lights.

"It'd be good," he said.

He produced some wire from his utility shed. There was a plastic drop cloth out there too, and we stretched it over the sofa in case the rain, which had stopped, started up again.

When I was done with the wiring, I found Dove in the kitchen. He put a beer in my hand and I sat down at the kitchen table. It was a nice maple table with not a crumb on it, only one clean ashtray and the pepper and salt shakers, like in a diner. Then he went to the refrigerator and pulled out some bread and baloney and started making sandwiches. "I'm deeply sorry I don't have nothing better to offer you," he said.

"Oh bullshit," I said.

Then I wondered if he was serious.

"Is that baloney? I like baloney," I said.

"It's all right," he said.

He was methodical. He laid out eight slices of bread and applied mayonnaise to four and mustard to four. I looked away, because it seemed like a private ritual. When the plates were finished. each one held two sandwiches and a green pickle spear. He saw me staring at the pickle spear and said, "Eat all you want of them pickles, because they're staying behind."

I said "Thank you" and got two more, and another beer at Dove's suggestion. I asked him what time he was leaving for Mississippi.

"Seven o'clock in the morning," he said.

"You're pulling that trailer to Mississippi with your truck?"

"Yes, Wendell. That's what I'm by golly going to do."

"Do you think you'll make it all right?"

"I expect to have a heart attack and kick the bucket. But I could do that watching television, too."

"Your television is at McInturff's," I said.

He took an enormous bite of baloney sandwich. I had never seen him eat food in all the time we had sat around drinking. He bit off a third of the sandwich at one go.

"Who's going with you?" I said.

"Nobody."

We ate quietly. I thought about Mary and wondered what she would be doing on our second night apart. Dove asked me, "Are you going to call Mary or not?" I said, "Not." He got up and walked down the hall, and in a few minutes I heard him snoring. It was maybe seven o'clock, not yet dark outside.

I set the remainder of my beer, most of a bottle, in the refrigerator along with Dove's second baloney sandwich. I went into the living room and sat down on the clean new carpet behind the coffee table, where the sofa had been, and I studied the portable telephone, trying to decide whether I would sound drunk if I called Mary. I didn't feel drunk so much as tired. Then I decided I didn't care how I sounded, because I needed to talk to her.

I called and got the answering machine. I said, "Mary, it's me, and I'm at Dove's, in case you wonder. I was thinking two things. First, is there any way you might hold off on that lawyer tomorrow? Second, is there any way if I come home you won't leave, so we can talk? If you're there, answer the phone."

I waited until the answering machine shut off, and then I called back and left Dove's phone number in case she wanted to call. Then I hung up and felt miserable. I got the rest of my beer from the refrigerator and drank it and ate the last baloney sandwich, my third.

I got up and washed the knife that Dove had used to spread the mustard and mayonnaise, and I balanced it at the edge of the sink to dry. I threw away the paper plates. Then I picked up a newspaper out of one of the kitchen chairs and found a new *Playboy* under it, and I sat down and looked through the *Playboy*, which made me feel great about myself and my whole life as it stood, and also my prospects for the future. I thought about my older sister, who is, believe it or not, an attorney in Atlanta, and what she would have said if she could have seen me. I imagined her saying "Yuck."

Then Dove came in with his shoes off, his shirt untucked, and his hair messed up. He wore his hair rather long but always neatly parted, combed, and sprayed—I may not have mentioned this before,. but he was a somewhat fastidious person concerning his appearance. He said, "There's clean towels in the bathroom, Wendell."

So I got up and took a shower. I didn't have anything to shave with, but at least I got clean, which was good. Then I put my dirty clothes back on.

Then I wandered back into the kitchen and found Dove flipping through the *Playboy*. I started to turn and go into the other room, but he said, "Come on in, ain't nothing going on in here." He kept turning pages, though, as I sat down. Then he sat back and lit a cigarette and said, "It's a shame—I can't get excited about any of that." He flipped his hand at the magazine.

I stared at a picture of a naked lady, upside down.

Then I glanced at Dove, and he was looking at me. He looked away.

I said, "I hope you're not about to tell me how your uncle used to touch you when you were little."

He said, "No, it was my aunt. I didn't mind it none."

We sat a while longer, and I said, "Do you need help driving tomorrow?"

He nodded slowly. "I'll take whatever help is offered."

"Just wake me up."

He showed me what room to sleep in. There was a chair, a dresser with a mirror, a picture of a log cabin on the wall, and on the floor, a blanket and a sheet neatly folded with a pillow on top. Dove said, "You and Mary don't have kids, do you, Wendell?"

"No."

"Don't never have kids," he said. "It ain't worth the heartache."

That wasn't an issue for us, I told him.

"You already decided that, did you?"

"It was decided for us, actually." Mary had been pregnant once, around the time we bought our house, but that had ended in a miscarriage. We later went to specialists, but nothing happened, and nothing was going to. Dove got all the facts out of me by direct questioning. He asked could we not have a test-tube baby, and I said that to try it would cost more than I normally made in a year.

He considered that. I was standing in the middle of the room in my socks, pants, and shirt, and he was at the doorway.

"You need to get up off your ass and start making more money," he said.

"Okay, Dove. Thanks for giving me that idea."

"No wonder she's mad. You could be building houses instead of cootering about like you do. Building houses is where the money's at."

"I guess I'll go to bed now," I said.

He stood glowering awhile, and then he said, "Well, shit, Wendell."

"Shit, Dove."

He backed out and shut the door, and I spread out the bedding and switched off the light and lay down.

8

DOVE WOKE ME UP AT SIX SAYING, "Come and eat some
damn breakfast, Wendell." I went into the kitchen and found
him frying baloney for sandwiches. It was better, fried.

Then we left. He said the truck was tricky to start first thing
in the morning, so he got behind the wheel and closed the
choke and fluttered the pedal in the particular way that was
required, and then the engine roared and we took off without
waiting to let it warm up. I questioned him on the latter point,
and he said you couldn't let the truck warm up or it would die.
"That's a problem," I said, and he said, "Not for me it ain't."

I asked Dove how many miles were on the truck, and he
said it had either 166,000 or 266,000. But the engine had been
gone through in recent memory. Also, it had a new set of used
tires on it. I asked why he didn't invest in a set of new tires and
he said, "Because they would only be ruined."

It was loud inside the truck. I could hear Dove all right
when he spoke because of his great deep voice, which had a
boom and a rattle to it so that I pictured the inside of his chest
as one of those old boiler rooms like on the *Lusitania* or somewhere, with rows of furnaces and great echoing spaces and bil-

lows of smoke and steam and men lying down dead of exhaustion. My own voice is of the normal range, and I had to raise it for him to hear me. We got on a hill on 36, also known as the Johnson City Highway in Kingsport or the Kingsport Highway if you are in Johnson City, and the truck started to strain. I said, "We may have to leave this horse trailer by the side of the road, Dove." He didn't answer, so I said, "We may have to leave this horse trailer by the road, Dove!"

"I heard you the first time, Wendell."

We got up the hill, and I decided I'd leave the worrying to him.

We came to the on-ramp for the freeway. It curved sharply and we took that part slow, and then we struggled to get up to freeway speed. We were doing about forty-five when Dove merged onto the four-lane, and he looked like his lips were going to pinch the filter in two on his cigarette. I imagined the lit end dropping off and starting a lap fire, which was a way for me to not think about the eighteen-wheelers coming up behind us doing eighty-nine miles per hour. Then the truck engine coughed and I said "Oh shit," but Dove didn't flinch, and then the engine smoothed out and started to sound better. Trucks and cars were passing us on the left, and one guy flipped us off, which made Dove finally smile. We hit fifty-five, and Dove said "Oh yeah, baby" in his most nasty and lascivious tone. He patted his truck on the dashboard.

Interstate 81 through this region is a pretty drive. You go past mountains and farms, and at a distance everything looks perfect. A house that you notice is clean and white, the roof is silver or green, the kitchen garden makes a nice rectangle with even rows, and maybe there will be a line of irises and a hose coiled on its rack neatly. The sight of it is pleasing. Also I love this feeling first thing in the morning when you are awake but still sleepy, so your brain is kind of dreamy and susceptible, and you're drinking coffee (Dove had brought us a thermos) and going somewhere, and the world is passing outside your window and you can take it all in and think your thoughts. I wished Mary was there, because if she had been I could have pointed at a house and said, "That's a nice place, isn't it?" and she'd have said, "Yes, it makes me want to go home and weed," and I'd have said, "Me too."

I suppose I could have said some of these things to Dove, but he was not who I wanted to be saying them to.

And then I thought, Why Mary? Why does it have to be this one person and not anybody else? Partly because I know her, I thought, and I know what I can say to her and what she will say back. Then also, it's because she surprises me, and I don't know what she will say.

I missed her so much that I didn't miss her. It was like she was there. I couldn't look out the window and see a cat hopping through tall grass without thinking of Mary's reaction to that, which would have been to laugh. And then I would laugh too, and right then I did. Therefore even though I should have been miserable, and was, in the truck that morning on my way with Dove to Hattiesburg, Mississippi to deliver some furniture, I was also in another way not miserable. I had a feeling of expectancy as though I was on a summer vacation that I would soon be back from. Then I would be with Mary again and tell her my adventures, and she'd tell me hers, and all would be right.

And then I thought, But it's Monday, and Mary is seeing a lawyer today.

I looked back at the sofa in the truck bed. The plastic drop cloth we had used to cover it was gone, blown off somewhere between where we were and Kingsport. I'd forgotten to secure it. I tried to make myself conceive the possibility that Mary and I might split up permanently and get a divorce. I couldn't do it. It was too weird a thing to imagine, like if somebody had said, "The earth will be a barren coal someday." I would say back, "Is that so? Now shut up and let me eat my chili bun."

It had become foggy. We were crossing the Holston River, but you couldn't see the water down below us for the mist that was under the bridge. Dove had both hands on the wheel and was leaning forward peering out the windshield. The wipers streaked the glass as much as they cleared it. Then I heard him jerk his foot and say "Oh oh oh," and I looked up and there were brake lights up ahead getting closer. Traffic was stopped. I stuck my coffee cup between my legs and fumbled for the seat belt in a great hurry, because Dove was taking forever to stop the truck. He was stopping it as fast as he could, but the trailer was pushing us.

We certainly would have slammed into the car ahead of us except that right before we got to it, it crept forwards again. We stopped safely, and I gave up hunting for the seat belt.

We did some swearing and then I poured Dove some coffee. He lit up another cigarette and cracked his window about two inches for the smoke to go out, which some small portion of it did do. On my side the crank for the window was missing, so I couldn't roll my window down, but I was able to filter most of the smoke out of the air using my lungs.

Traffic barely moved. We got off the bridge but were still in fog. We stopped dead and some time went by, and then somebody came walking past Dove's window to the car ahead of us and talked to the driver. I thought, I'm glad we didn't cream that car.

Then we'd roll a few yards forwards again. This went on a long time, until Dove started bouncing side to side like a baby bird and hissing profanities. "What?" I said. He leaned over me to look into the mirror on my side, and then he pulled off onto the right shoulder.

"What in the heck is the problem?" I said.

He jabbed his finger at the temperature gauge that was mounted under the dash. It was pegged at about 240. "Hadn't you better stop?" I said.

"Because we're stopped is why it's hot," he said. We drove on down the shoulder of the highway passing everybody, and the engine temperature went down a little then bounced back up. I turned the heater on full blast, and that helped. Luckily we were near an exit, and we were able to get off and stop at an Exxon.

We asked if there was a hose, and the woman who was sweeping the pavement said they didn't have one. I had Mary's Exxon card with me, so I used it to buy an eight-dollar gallon of antifreeze. We added this to the radiator, then topped it off with water carried from the men's room.

Then we had a choice: get back on the interstate, which the woman who was sweeping said was backed up all the way to Knoxville because of construction, or go another route, like U.S. 11. Eleven was twenty miles out of our way, but we agreed we would rather drive the wrong direction than creep and stop like we had been. So we got back in the truck with Dove driving again and set off toward 11.

The truck ran okay now and didn't overheat. Dove admitted he had been knowing for a long time that coolant was leaking from one of the core plugs but had forgotten to top it off before we left, and I cussed him staunchly, which made him feel better, I think. The fog burned off. We were on an old curvy two-lane that followed between the hills like a creek, rather than cutting straight through as a new road would do. We passed a barn whose corner was right up against the road, and it had an old Kern's Bread sign on it, and Dove started telling me about how the country stores used to be, back when he was a boy. He described going into a store barefooted and buying cheese and crackers. The crackers were saltines, the square perforated into four smaller squares—I also remembered these—and in the store they were kept in a glass jar on the counter.

Then he told about his mother, who had died not that long ago in the nursing home where she had lived for many years, and how as a young woman she had been notorious for getting into cars with men. It was because she loved to go for drives. I tried to picture that—Dove's mother in 1930, riding around in somebody's car and stopping at a little store to get a sandwich made of two perforated saltine crackers with a slice of cheese in the middle.

I told Dove I liked saltines when they were fresh and would snap apart. If you wrapped the cheese and crackers to eat them later, the crackers would get soft, which I didn't like. He knew what I meant and concurred at a great volume. I then wondered to myself whether Dove's mother had been a lively and/or attractive person back in 1930, when she was twenty or so. I figured yes, because most twenty-year-old women are both, when you come right down to it.

As though he had read my mind Dove said, "My old mama was a good-looking woman in her day."

9

WE MEANDERED AND MEANDERED and at length reached
Greeneville, which was not encouraging since Greeneville
should have been an hour's drive from where we started, and
we'd been gone more like three hours. We got on U.S. 11,
though, and made better time. We passed back over the interstate and saw to our satisfaction that traffic in the southbound
lanes was dead still.

We stayed on 11 through Morristown and various small
communities, poking along catching every other red light and
taking in the scenery, which included lots of cows and coin-
operated car washes, and the interesting motor hotels from the
days before the freeway, some with the plate glass knocked out
and shrubbery growing inside the rooms, and others that were
still doing a little business, though who would choose to stay in
one of them out here in the middle of no place particular was
another question.

We drove through downtown Knoxville and passed my
granddad's old plumbing-supply shop, which he'd sold when I
was a boy. I had memories of rolling a toy truck in the aisles.
Dove did not mind in the least to hold up traffic at a busy inter-

section while he waited for a gap that suited him so he could make a nice, wide, easygoing left-hand turn across multiple lanes. I was glad I had gone to the trouble of causing the trailer lights to work. I had not taken this route through the city in some time, and I thought about my parents again and wondered what I'd say to them if Mary did go through with what she was threatening.

By the time we got across Knoxville we were hungry for lunch. We stopped at a McDonald's and I ran in and got us some food. Dove was on the passenger side when I got back, so I drove and ate.

He had taken two bites of his hamburger when he looked at it and said, "This is simply awful." He wrapped it up in the paper and put it back in the sack. Then he opened the glove compartment, took out a window crank and placed it on the stem in the passenger door, rolled down the window, and threw the sack out of the truck.

"What in the hell did you do that for?" I said.

He didn't say anything. He looked as though he wanted to throw up.

"There was another hamburger in there," I said.

"I know it. That's why I put it out the window."

"I don't approve of throwing trash out the window," I said.

"The convicts will pick it up."

Still, it brought me down, and I continued to tell him what a bad thing he had done until he said, "Well turn it back around and we'll get my sack, crybaby."

I ignored him then.

"Turn it around!" he said.

He wouldn't let up until finally I got so tired of hearing him that I picked up my own sack out of the floor and threw it out my window. That satisfied him and he was quiet.

It made me feel worse, though.

I have often noticed this about long trips—you can drive for a couple hours and be loving life, and then for the next couple hours you wish you were dead. I guess it's something about being shut inside a small box for a length of time.

I didn't wish I was dead, but I didn't like what all was happening. Also, it was getting quite warm in the truck, which did not have air-conditioning. We rode a long time without talking, and then Dove said, "Up here on the right I would like you to stop at this store, please sir."

It was a little beer and bait shop. Dove went in and came out with a twelve-pack of Natural Light in bottles. This was well enough, but as soon as we started moving again he said, "Let's find where we're staying tonight, Wendell."

I said, "I thought we were going to Mississippi."

He slid a bottle into his foam-rubber bottle holder, which had been riding up front with us on the bench seat the whole way. He said, "I can't set in this truck much longer, Wendell. I'll die."

I told him I was low on cash and hadn't expected to pay for a room.

"You probably need to buy you some fresh drawers," he said.

He was right. We drove another two hours and stopped in Chattanooga, which was about halfway to where we were going. Dove directed me to a place called the Scotty Inn and had me park the truck and trailer crossways at the front of the lot, taking up five spaces. I objected and we argued about it, but then I realized I didn't actually care but was only tired, so I did what he said. Dove went in and got us a room, and we walked down to the other end of the building and went in it.

It had two double beds and one of the walls was made of

plywood, and it was very small and smelled like the devil. Dove expressed his disgust and then he set himself up on the bed with his beers and two packs of Cambridge cigarettes and the remote control, and seemed at home except that he said I might need to go get more beer in a little while.

I went out into the parking lot in the sunlight and started walking. I got the idea I would walk until I found a place where I could buy some underwear and socks, and then I would charge them on my Visa check card, which comes directly out of the checking account, and then I would call Mary and tell her the amount so she could deduct it from the checkbook register. This gave me something to look forward to, and I felt better.

I pretended Mary was there and felt close to her. There was no sidewalk—this was an outskirts-of-town spot where the highway was several lanes across, and I walked from parking lot to parking lot, past car dealerships and a doughnut shop. On the ground I saw a bird that had died and a lot of pieces of wire and trash. Between paved areas, the grass was tall.

I came to a shopping center with a Dollar General in it, and I bought a pack of Fruit of the Looms, some tube socks, a green short-sleeved shirt, and some long pants. I then went to a pay phone and dialed 1–800-COLLECT. It gave me the *brring* sound and then I had to say my name and so on, but Mary didn't answer. The 1–800-COLLECT computer asked if I wanted to leave a message, and I hung up.

10

I WALKED BACK TO THE SCOTTY INN. I had not thought to bring the key, so I had to knock and at first wondered if Dove might be dead because he took so long to get to the door. He had only been asleep.

He had put the beer in the sink and covered it with ice. I had a couple with him then took a shower, then put on some of my new underwear and socks. Everything seemed a tiny bit better then. The old underclothes were consigned to the wastebasket.

I went back out and tried Mary again and got ahold of her this time. I told her I had some amounts she needed to write in the checkbook register. My heart was thumping so hard I could feel it in my ears. I'm not exaggerating. I asked her did she have a pen handy. All of this came out in a burst as soon as she answered the phone.

She told me to wait, and then she said, "Okay, I'm ready."

I told her the amounts for the Dollar General and for a couple other receipts I had been carrying in my wallet, and then I asked her what the balance was. It was something like three hundred dollars.

I asked her if she had gone to the lawyer today, and she said yes she had. I asked what they had come up with and she said, "Nothing much, yet."

"What does that mean?"

"I found out what all the steps are, but I haven't started it yet."

It seemed to me that going to the lawyer was equivalent to starting it, but I didn't say so. I was all keyed up, on an edge between pissed off and scared and wanting to go home and beg. I stood there with my head flashing and then she asked me where I was.

"Chattanooga," I said.

Now she was quiet. I started explaining about Dove and his daughter and moving the furniture. "I was hoping you'd call me at Dove's last night. That's why I left the number."

"I thought you wanted to come home," she said.

"I do."

"Then why are you in Chattanooga?"

"Well you never called back," I said. I could feel where this was going, and it wasn't good. I told her, "Look, I'll come home right now."

"No, don't come," she said.

But I said I would, and then she said, "I won't be here." Then I said, "Okay, I won't come home. You stay there."

Then neither of us said anything for a long time, and then she said "Bye" and hung up.

I went back to the room. Dove knew that I had called her, and he asked me how it went. I told him what happened and that I shouldn't have called, because now I didn't know whether she would stay at the house or not. I wasn't sure how we had left it. He said, "Hang in there, bud-ro."

We drank the rest of the beer, and I went out and got more

of it and a bucket of chicken. We watched *Dragnet,* and Dove had some things to say about how Joe Friday walks and why he might walk that way. We liked Joe Friday, though. Dove unpacked his medicine bottles onto the bathroom counter. There were six or seven different pills and sprays and things that he used. Then he cleaned out his ashtray and adjusted the air conditioner, and then he smoked one more cigarette over the sink, and then we turned off the lights and he went to sleep, I guess. I couldn't. I lay awake for a couple of hours feeling tired but not sleepy, and then this dog got to barking outside and about drove me crazy. It kept on and wouldn't stop. Well, finally I decided I was going out and find that dog and kill it with a rock.

It was 2:02 A.M. I put my pants and shoes on and got the key and went out, and there was the dog, out loose and barking at the gate of a fenced-in area where the trash was kept behind the Breakfast House restaurant, next door to our end of the motel. The gate was chained, but the chain was only looped around, not locked, so I said What the heck and I opened the gate and let the dog run in.

There was some crashing and scrambling, and then the dog, who was a fairly large dog, came loping out happily from the garbage pen with a pale furry thing in his jaws that was about the size of a deflated football. The dog jogged towards the motel, and damn if he didn't stop right almost in front of the door to our room and drop whatever it was on the walkway there.

I ran the dog off and saw that the thing he had got was a possum. Its mouth was open with a long row of small, snarly teeth and a narrow pink tongue showing. There was a spot of blood on its fur where the dog had clamped on.

I don't like possums. Their bald tails give me the creeps. I was unhappy now because the possum lay right by our door, and I knew I was going to want to move it before I went back into the room and tried to sleep. I also knew I didn't have a shovel or even a big stick handy to move it with, and I don't go in for touching dead animals with my hands.

I stood for some time in the pinkish light from the parking-lot floods. The possum was plump and had straight, oily-looking gray fur and a pointed snout. Its black eyes were open. I thought, How depressing, to be an ugly, dirty little beast with a life of running up and down the roads all night, trying to do things for yourself and hiding I don't know where in the daytime, and then one night you're sorting through some trash in apparent safety and this shirtless joker lets in a dog that wants to crack your spine for the hell of it, and you're dead.

I wished I had stayed out of this. For that matter, I wished I had never wound up at the Scotty Inn of Chattanooga.

I wandered at the edge of the parking lot looking for a stick or anything rigid with which to move the possum. The murdering dog followed me. We wandered rather far afield, back behind the Breakfast House and beyond it to a car lot. Finally I found a piece of automobile trim at the edge of the road, and we made our way back to the room.

It appeared that the possum had come back to life, because now it was gone.

11

I WENT BACK TO BED and after a long time, morning came. I felt like my skeleton was made out of emery boards.

We went to the Breakfast House. We sat in a booth. The waitress was sixteen, judging by her looks, and she was angry with the world, and Dove and myself being part of the world she was angry with us as well. I still hadn't shaved and I was wearing my green shirt from Dollar General, and I probably wasn't a pretty sight. Dove wasn't pretty either, but at least he had shaved and combed his hair and was sitting up straight. That's one thing I will give him—he always looked as good as he knew how to.

Anyway, she slung her hips up to the table and put her pen tip to the pad and didn't say anything, just looked at Dove like he was absolutely the most boring idiot that providence had ever made the mistake of placing on earth. Dove said in his booming voice, with a grave frown, "Who are you?"

She grabbed her name tag, which was pinned to her dress, and aimed it at him. She said, "What'll you have?"

He studied her for a second, and then he said, "Who's fixing it?"

"The man at the grill with his back to you."

Dove rubbed his forehead. She turned to me and asked if I knew what I wanted.

"I want some black coffee."

Her eyelids fluttered and she said, "Do you want cream?"

"No, I'll take it black."

"I'll have the same thing," Dove said. "Except I don't want any cream with mine."

She walked away.

I said to Dove, "At least I know somebody feels worse than I do."

He said in a low voice, or as low as he could make his go, "I'll tell you this, Wendell. Do you know what she's doing right now?"

"Getting our coffee?"

"Spitting in it."

In a minute, here she came from a swinging door behind the counter carrying two mugs by the handles. She put them on a tray and poured coffee into them.

"Now then," Dove said. "Why did she bring them mugs from the back, when there's stacks of them next to the coffeemaker?"

"I don't think she spit in them," I said.

She brought us our coffee along with a handful of creamers. She gave Dove a pretty smile and said, "What's for breakfast?"

"What are you smiling for?" Dove said.

"What?"

She had small, square, even teeth. Her skin had a flat look. I wondered what day of the week it was and realized it was Tuesday. Why was she not in school? Then I remembered it was summer. It was about seven-thirty A.M., though, which seemed early to have to be at work, for a kid on summer break.

Dove glared at his menu and said, "I ain't having nothing."

"Not anything?" she said.

"No! And I advise you don't, Wendell." He set the menu down and got out a cigarette.

I said, "I'll have two fried eggs, bacon, hash browns, and toast."

Dove asked if they had cereal in sealed boxes.

"Yes we do," she said.

"What about a container of milk that ain't been opened?"

"You mean an individual milk?"

"Right."

"No, it comes out of a dispenser."

"Well have you got bananas?"

"Yes."

"I want two bananas , and that's all. I'll peel them myself."

She wrote that down and left.

Dove settled back shaking his head and told me quietly, "You have to be vigilant in a hole like this."

I told him I had a strong constitution and some little girl's spit would not harm me, especially if I was none the wiser.

"That's your problem exactly," he said. "You are none the wiser."

I had a laugh over that.

He asked me if I made a habit of running in and out of doors all through the night. No, I said, and I told him about the possum pretending it was dead. He said, "Do you know some people eats them dirty sons of bitches?"

"I wouldn't eat one," I said.

"You'll eat worse here in a minute," he said. Then he went into a discussion of hepatitis C, which he said I could expect to catch from the waitress's saliva. It would eventually kill me.

That started to worry me, or it started to start to—anyway, to settle it I drank some of my coffee.

"There, it's done," I said.

"It's done!"

She brought out my food and Dove's bananas on a plate. I said something to her about how she must have come in pretty dadgone early, and was she in school, and she said she didn't mind coming in early and no, she wasn't in school. I decided, listening to her talk, that she was older than I had thought before. She said, "I work here five-thirty to eleven, and then I go home and sleep, and then I work my other job in the evening."

"What's your other job?" Dove asked her.

"Telemarketing."

"You might remember me then," he said. "I'm the one that says *Click.*"

And then I don't remember how we got around to this, but she was going on and mentioned that the previous night she had been trying to change a lightbulb in her apartment and fell off a box, hit her head, and knocked herself out.

"What kind of box?" Dove said.

"A cardboard box."

"I could have told you not to do that, honey."

"I know," she said. She put her hand up to her head and moved her fingers lightly.

"How long was you out?" Dove asked her.

"I think for a few minutes—" Then she stopped and said never mind, she didn't want to disgust us before we ate.

Dove pressed her, though, and she explained that she thought she had been out for several minutes, because when she finally sat up there was drool all down her cheek.

She laughed softly.

Dove said, "Don't you live with nobody?"

"Only my friend Mr. Browning Nine Millimeter."

Dove popped back in his seat as though he was shocked, and then he busted out into his enormous tree-felling laugh. The waitress gave me an Is He Crazy look and I said, "He likes to be put in his place."

"Oh, one of those," she said. Then she sat down at a booth by the far wall and lit a cigarette and started rolling up silverware in paper napkins.

After we got through the breakfast and paid for it (by the time we left, Dove was fast friends with this waitress, and I don't see how he managed it but I saw him do it many times— he would win people over through obnoxiousness) we went back towards the room, which was only a few steps from where we ate. Dove said, "Do you notice anything different about the truck, Wendell?"

I looked across the parking lot to where we'd left it. "Where's the horse trailer?"

"Evidently someone has stole it."

"Oh shit!" I said.

I ran over. Dove walked. The truck was as we'd left it, with the sofa still in the bed. Everything was the same, as far as I could tell, except that the trailer was missing.

"Well shit, did they do it while we were eating just now?" I said.

"It was done last night," Dove said.

"I can't believe we didn't notice it when we walked out for breakfast."

"I noticed it," he said.

"You noticed it before we went in the restaurant?"

"Yes."

"Why didn't you say anything?"

"Would it have made any difference?"

"I would say that the sooner we call the police, the likelier you are to have your trailer and furniture back."

He frowned at me and said, "Wendell, you're naive."

"What are you talking about, Dove?"

"We're not getting that trailer back. It's gone. Let's get in the truck and leave, and maybe we'll get to Hattiesburg at a decent hour."

I considered all of this. Then I turned and headed for the motel office to call the police.

"Wendell," Dove said.

"What?"

"Let's go on."

I stood and considered it again. It didn't make sense to not call the police. On the other hand, who was I to try to talk an old man into reporting his stolen trailer load of furniture if he didn't want to? I had my own heartaches to tend without adopting his as well. So I acquiesced, and he gave me the keys, and we got in the truck and drove out of Chattanooga.

12

STILL I COULDN'T LET IT GO. Something was wrong, because you do not load up a trailer with your own furniture to haul it five hundred miles to give away, and then, when somebody steals it, shrug and say Oh well. After we had driven awhile in silence—I think we had already crossed into Georgia, which you cut through a corner of after leaving Chattanooga—oh, and we were on the freeway now, because the truck drove immensely better without the trailer behind it—I said, "Whose trailer was that, Dove?"

"Jennifer Mickle's ex-husband's."

"Who is Jennifer Mickle?"

"Steve Mickle's girl."

"Aren't Steve Mickle and all of them going to be sorry they let you use it, when they find out it got stolen and we didn't even call the police?"

"Hell no. You see, Wendell, the boy left it at Steve Mickle's place, and Mickle has been trying to get him to come and get it for two years. So he told me to take it, and he's telling Rod that it was stolen out of his barn. It all works out good, see?"

"What about your furniture that was in it?"

"I don't really give a *scheiss* about that, Wendell."

"Okay. Well that explains what we're doing here on this whole trip, then."

He took a big suck of breath and turned to face me in the seat, and he started doing the baby-bird dance. "Well right there's the door, Wendell! Just pull this truck over and hop out! Pull it over!"

He was loud. I ducked, he was so loud.

I said, "Damn, Dove. Don't get mad."

I watched him for a second and I swear, I thought he was going to hit me. I took it seriously because Dove was the kind of man who, no matter how physically feeble he was, if he was unhappy with you he would make you feel it. His eyes got wet and he looked like his head was ready to pop.

"Shit, Dove. Look, we'll drop it."

Then he sulled up.

We rode and made good time. As I said, you cut a corner of Georgia, and then very shortly you find yourself in Alabama, driving a long ways through nothing much but trees and low hills. In Gadsden we had a bad experience at a drive-through window where the girl took forever and then got our order wrong and asked us to pull over and park. She said they would have to bring our order to us in the parking lot, because we had "timed out."

"What in the hell are you saying?" Dove hollered from the passenger side, and I thought to myself, Here we go. She explained that they had a certain amount of time in which to handle each drive-through customer at the window, and we had gone past ours. "Whose son-of-a-bitching fault is that?" Dove inquired. Then the drive-through girl said, "I will not speak with an abusive customer." I wanted to leave then, but Dove was determined we were going to sit there and nobody else was getting anything until we had our food, and had it like we wanted it. I killed the engine, because even though the girl was right that Dove was being a tad bit abusive, Dove was also somewhat right that it was not our fault we timed out. It was a relief to let the shuddering engine go quiet. It had a miss, which was most pronounced at idle. I noticed what a pleasant day it was. It was warm and quite bright out, but the air was moving some. I looked across the road to a Burger King where I wished we had gone, and there was a playground in front of it and a small boy standing on top of a climbing fort there, with his hands on the rail, looking out towards the traffic and the day like a little king surveying his world.

After Gadsden you bypass Birmingham. Then you bypass Tuscaloosa. Then you drive and drive, and then you come into Mississippi past a big antebellum-looking welcome sign with white columns and magnolia blossoms painted on it. There was a second sign which said ONLY POSITIVE MISSISSIPPI SPOKEN HERE. I pointed that out to Dove and he said, "Well, bless their hearts." We had gotten into the beer by now, and he was in a better mood than before.

You come into Meridian, which has about four exits, and then you go through Laurel. We were tired, and in Laurel I almost ran off the road where it bends suddenly on a bridge in the middle of town. I got it back together, though. We saw a sign for Hattiesburg. We stopped at a Texaco, and Dove went to the pay phone to call his daughter and get directions. She wasn't home.

We drove another half hour not talking, then took an exit for Hattiesburg. Where we emerged was a very congested seven- or eight-lane stretch of road with traffic signals every quarter mile. It was the Kmart and Wal-Mart area of town. We went into a Mexican restaurant in the parking lot of a Sack

and Save grocery store and got a beer, and Dove told me that
when he called he had spoken to his grandson.

"Did you get directions?" I said.

"He's six," Dove said. "He don't know how to get there."

"And he's home by himself?"

"Yes, and he don't know when his mama will be back."

"Do you know any neighbors to call?"

"Hell no."

"Well do you even know her address?"

"I got it wrote down at home."

I went to the register to borrow a phone book. They didn't
want to give it to me to take back to the table but I told them
Dove could barely walk, and then they gave it to me.

"What's the last name?" I said.

"MacPherson."

I looked it up: Rhonda MacPherson, with an apartment
number on Pine Street. I showed it to Dove. "That's the place
she just moved out of," he said.

I took the phone book back to the register.

"Who do you know that would have her address?" I said
when I got back to our table.

"Her mother."

"Call her mother, then."

"There ain't no need to upset her mother," Dove said.

We ordered a pitcher and some food. I had a Mexican combination plate that was unobjectionable, and Dove got a pair of
tacos which he then did not eat, except for half of one of them.
He did not complain to the waiter but was polite. Then he
called again and got Rhonda this time, and we set off for her
house.

13

WE DROVE PAST IT TWICE. It was dark by now, and the house had no porch light on. There were no streetlights either. The road had brought us south past a Marshall Durbin chicken-processing plant, a water-treatment plant, and then woods, clay pits, and a school bus made over into a house. Across from Rhonda's was a long, plain cinder-block building with a flat roof and a sign out front with the Pabst Blue Ribbon logo. Under the logo in letters with too much space between them was the name of the bar, Gene's. Gene's was doing a little business.

Rhonda came out and met us in the yard after we pulled in. She hugged her father and he told her it would have been nice to have had the porch light on for us, and she said that the bulb was burned out, and he told her it needed to be replaced. He introduced us and we shook hands. She was tall. She asked me, "Did he drive you nuts?" I looked around in the dark to see where Dove was before I answered, and I couldn't find him.

"Not completely nuts," I said.

We went inside and I saw her in the light. She was more rugged-looking than in the picture Dove had showed me. Also, her hair was lighter now. It was long and coarse, held back in a clip, and she was barefooted and wearing jeans and a western-style shirt with about two of the snaps fastened and the loose ends knotted over her brown stomach. Not that this is relevant to anything, but her stomach looked like you could chop carrots on it. I thought of Mary's stomach, softer and white.

Rhonda hadn't said anything about the trailer not being there, so I said, "I guess Dove told you on the phone about the trailer getting stolen."

"What trailer?" she said.

Just then Dove walked in carrying a beer in his purple insulated beer-bottle holder.

Rhonda said, "Did you find the beer, Daddy?"

"I brought it with me," he said. He handed me the bottle and I twisted the cap off for him. He was capable of doing it himself, but I was faster. He threw back a headful and then wiped his bottom lip with his finger and said, "Where's the little boy at?"

"Hiding," Rhonda said.

Dove moaned. It was a big, loud moan, as from a man in agony. He said, "Where is he, down there?"—pointing down the hallway—and Rhonda nodded, and Dove went off that way muttering that he was going to fall over something and be dead.

Rhonda stared at me, and then she turned and went into the kitchen.

The house smelled musty. The living room, where I stood, contained a bookcase with a television and knickknacks in it and a sofa that was the near twin of the one in the back of Dove's truck. Behind a round dining-room-style table and some chairs was a collection of maybe thirty cardboard boxes blocking a patio door. On the floor, the carpet was worn to a matlike texture.

I thought, as I had many times before, that on balance we are better off without carpeting. Making things worse was the untidiness of the room. I reminded myself that these people had just moved in. When I'd had enough of standing by myself in the living room, I went into the kitchen, where Rhonda offered me one of our beers, which I accepted. She opened one for herself as well. We sat down at the table and she asked me about the trip. I realized that she did not understand this to be a furniture-delivering trip, like I did, but instead was thinking of it as simply a visit. This made me wonder whether she did not wonder what I was doing here. I didn't say anything else about the trailer or the furniture, leaving that to Dove.

She asked me, "How did he do on the drive?"

"Okay, I guess."

She nodded and took a good healthy Ellender draw on her beer. When she'd swallowed she said right out loud, "He looks like hell."

"He seems to be doing all right," I said.

"Compared to what?"

"I don't know. Compared to how he's usually doing."

She considered that, then gave a shrug. "Daddy's a case," she said.

There was a loud squeal from the back of the house, followed by a roar. A small boy came tearing into the kitchen. When he saw me, he stopped so quick he almost rolled. He gawked at me, and then he went to his mother's chair and said something in her ear. She said, "He's a friend of your grand-daddy's, Michael."

Michael said "Hi" and tore off again. He ran into Dove in the doorway and might have knocked him down, but Dove grabbed the wall in time. Michael said "Ow" then ran on. Dove let go of the wall and moved across the floor to the counter. He said to Rhonda, "What in hell was the boy doing in the house by himself, tell me?"

Rhonda pushed herself up out of her chair and asked me whether I wanted a sandwich.

Dove said, "The man just got done sitting in a restaurant for two hours, waiting on you to come home and answer the phone!"

"I was not out for two hours," Rhonda said. She pointed her finger at me, wanting an answer about the sandwich. I said, "No thanks." She said, "I went out for one hour to take Jimbo some supper."

"Can't he get his own supper? How old is the son of a bitch?"

"He couldn't leave work," she said. She was pulling things out of the refrigerator, and she hollered for Michael to come eat.

"You couldn't take the boy with you?"

"No. Jimbo wanted me to bring him, but there's too much going on over there."

"Hey Wendell, maybe you didn't know they sold cars after nine P.M. on a Tuesday. That's their busiest time, though."

"He's not selling cars right now. They're trying to fire him."

"What do you mean they're trying to fire him?"

"The manager tried to fire him this afternoon, and he's staying."

"Who's staying?"

"Jimbo is. He's not leaving."

She set down a jar of mayonnaise on the counter and turned around to face her father. Dove's cheeks had spots of magenta on them. He was about to go into baby bird.

Rhonda said, "Daddy, don't start with your crap!"

Michael came running in and took a chair beside me. I got

up to leave the kitchen and Dove said in a small, choking voice, "Stay put, Wendell." He took his beer with him into the living room.

Rhonda asked Michael if he wanted a ham sandwich. He said he wanted cereal, so she put down the sandwich, which was already made and which she had been about to set in front of him on a paper towel, and she took a yellow bowl from the cabinet and put some cereal and milk in it and set that in front of him. Then she picked up the sandwich and took a bite of it and carried it with her into the living room.

I got myself another beer from the refrigerator. I twisted the cap off and stood waiting for the yelling to begin in the other room, but it didn't. I heard them talking in normal tones. I couldn't tell what they said, but then, I wasn't quite trying to.

I watched Michael eat. He had on a striped T-shirt and pajama bottoms. The cereal he ate was Lucky Charms. He took it in by spoonfuls, I noticed. When my sister and I were kids and ate that cereal, we always picked out the marshmallow treats and ate them first. I asked him how old he was.

He started thumping on the table with his fist. I thought, This is just what I need, for this kid to wig out right this minute. It appeared that he was having either a seizure or a tantrum of some kind. But then I got it that he was counting out his age like a horse.

I had not been counting, so I said, "Do that again." He dropped his head and thumped again six times. Then he asked me how old I was, and I thumped on the countertop thirty-two times.

He rolled his eyes. I was ridiculously old to him.

He was done with his cereal, so I asked him if he wanted more. He said no, he wanted some Pepsi. "Isn't it a bit late for that?" I said. I told him the caffeine would keep him awake.

No, caffeine did not bother him, he said. "I always drink caffeine."

We looked at each other a little while.

Then he said, "We have caffeine-free Pepsi." I looked in the refrigerator and sure enough, the Pepsi was caffeine-free and sugar-free as well. I poured him a nice big tumblerful with ice, and I sat down with him at the table.

Rhonda and Dove came back in, at peace now. She set an ashtray on the table for Dove and he said, "No, I won't smoke in your house."

"Jimbo does," she said.

"He ought not to," Dove said. He sat down at the table and gave Michael a long scowl, and Rhonda came and stood behind Michael and stroked his hair. She had large hands like her father, and her fingernails were all filed evenly and were painted gold. She pulled her nails lightly through Michael's hair while she was talking, and he got a sleepy look. I did too, no doubt. She noticed Michael's glass then and said, "Are you drinking Pepsi?" She rocked his head a little between her hands, and Michael said with his eyes shut, "Wendell gave it to me."

14

MICHAEL WENT TO SLEEP in his chair and got carried off somewhere by Rhonda and put down for the night. Dove and I got more beers from the refrigerator. We drank and drank, and I felt it. On Dove, however, a few more beers never showed. He sat there quite serene, sipping and talking with his hair neatly combed as always. He did give in and light up a cigarette once Michael had been dispatched.

I told Dove he was lizardlike because he rarely ate and could sit in one place for hours. He didn't care—he started flicking his tongue like a reptile, and Rhonda called him "Iguanodon."

The subject of sleeping arrangements came up, and I was told I would have Michael's bed. I asked Dove where he was sleeping, and Rhonda said, "Daddy's sleeping on the couch in the den." I said no, Dove should have the bed, and he said, "I am taking the couch and there will be no more discussion of it." Well, I was not the man to try and erode his strong ideals just then, so I said, "Okay, thank you," and hobbled off down the hallway to go to bed. I do not actually remember getting into the bed but I know that I did, and I fell hard asleep.

Somewhat later I woke up and was wide awake. I had no
sense of how long I had been there or what time it was. I was
hot, and I had a ghastly taste in my mouth and felt like vomit-
ing. The thought of this made me despair, because nobody
wants to have to vomit in someone else's house.

Many thoughts were in my brain, and they weren't the
happy or logical daytime sorts of thoughts but the troubled,
lying-awake kind. I wanted to go back to sleep, but I couldn't. I
couldn't stop noticing the unpleasant smell in the room. This
was a cinder-block house, and they're known to sweat in a
humid climate like we were in. The sweat fosters mildew
growth inside the walls and along the floors.

I myself was not fresh-smelling, having driven several
hours in the hot pickup the day before and not bathed since.

I thought about Mary and was miserable. I had a sudden
revelation of something that when I thought about it for a
minute seemed very obvious: of course Mary and I would not
get back together. I had been hoping all this time, either in the
back of my mind or in the front of it, that when I got back
from this trip I would go to the house and she'd be there and
we'd talk and make adjustments and then things would go
back to what they'd been before. How stupid of me to suppose
that, I thought. It is over and both of us know it.

And yet the more immediate thing that was making me
unhappy was not knowing whether I would have to get out of
the bed and go throw up. In my black-hearted, wee-hours
frame of mind I decided the best thing would be to slip out the
front door and wander off down the road somewhere to get
sick. That way no one would hear me or know it. I sweltered
some more, worried, hated myself, and so on for a while longer;
then I got up and put on my pants, shirt, and shoes. I got my
toothbrush and opened the bedroom door quietly. But just at

that moment the hall light came on, and Rhonda was there in a bathrobe and slippers with her hair down and squinting at me. She rubbed at her face and said, "Hey. Good morning."

"Good morning," I said.

"The coffee'll be ready in a minute," she said, and she went past me towards the kitchen.

I changed my plan and went on down to the bathroom to wash my face. My hands trembled, as they do sometimes after I drink too much. I got a glimpse of myself in the mirror, and it wasn't nice—not that it's ever all that nice, but right now it was especially unpleasant. The need to vomit went away, however. I brushed my teeth.

Sleeping any more did not seem likely, so I went to the kitchen. Rhonda was at the counter with her back to me, and here is something stupid—I felt a rush of strong affection for her. I don't mean I wanted to do anything to her—it was something more distant than that. Maybe I was wanting to pretend that I was at home, and that Rhonda was Mary, though she didn't look anything like Mary, even with her back turned. Mary's hair is darker and her shoulders are more square, and also the bathrobe that Rhonda was wearing was not one I could picture Mary in. It was pink and of a velourlike material. There was not a thing in the world wrong with it nor with Rhonda, but I am just saying everything's different. Anyway, Rhonda turned and I saw her nose from the side for a second, and saw the slight hook or bend in it, and liked her.

She set me down a cup of coffee on the table, and I sat down behind it. I asked her what she was doing up at this hour and she said she always got up about now because Michael would be awake soon and shouting, and she liked to get some coffee before that started. I gathered it was not the middle of the night, as I'd thought, but sometime close to morning. I asked her whether she worked, and she said she had quit her job for the summer because she could not make enough anyway to hardly pay a baby-sitter. Jimbo had been making good money, at least until yesterday, she said.

She was putting away dishes from the drying rack. She asked me did my wife and I have kids.

"No," I said.

She asked if we wanted to.

For whatever reason I didn't dodge the question, as I normally do when asked it, but told her, "Yes, we want to."

She folded the drying rack and hung it on a hook on the wall. She poured herself some coffee and sat down across from me. She said, "How old is your wife?"

"Thirty-two."

"Mm." She rubbed at her eye, and then she looked at me and frowned a little and said, "What are you waiting on?"

I told her we weren't waiting, and I told her about the miscarriage and so on. She nodded and looked off at the wall.

I found that strange. The reason that ordinarily I avoid discussing this business with people is that I dread the cooing and sympathy, and the awkwardness. I don't want to make people feel embarrassed, and I certainly don't want to feel embarrassed myself or to have people feel sorry for Mary and me. But evidently I did expect and desire Rhonda's sympathy, because I found myself feeling put out with her when she stared at the wall and said nothing. Her lack of any reaction surprised me and made me mad.

Then I thought how stupid I was.

Then Rhonda scraped her chair back to one side and said, "Well, that baby is out there somewhere."

"What do you mean?" I said. I didn't know what she was talking about.

"I mean he's out there," she said. She said it simply but with conviction, as though she was speaking about the Bigfoot.

I said, "No, it was a miscarriage. Mary never had the baby."

"There was still a baby, though," Rhonda said.

"There was something, but I don't know if it was a baby yet."

"How far along was she?"

"Two months."

"There was a baby at two months," she said. "You know there was."

"I know it?"

"Yes, you know it."

"No, I don't know it," I said.

"Haven't you ever looked at a book about babies?"

"I've seen pamphlets."

"Well when do you think there is a baby? At what time?"

"I don't know," I said. "Not at two months."

She sniffed and drank some coffee. I didn't like her tone. She was matter-of-fact, as though she owned this topic and nobody knew anything about it besides herself. She said, "People are having babies at five months now and they live."

"Not us."

"Do you believe that people have souls?"

I put my hands up and pushed them at her to say *Whoa.*

"Look, be honest," she said.

"I don't know if people have souls," I said. "I don't worry about that."

"You don't worry about that?"

"Right."

"I don't believe you," she said. "Everybody thinks about that."

And then, what happened to me was I partly wanted to argue with her, and I partly didn't, and I solved it by just giving up and not caring. I said, "Okay, you don't believe me. That's all right. But to me, what you're talking about is superstition."

"Superstition?"

"Superstition. Like ghosts and stuff."

She said, "Look, Wendell, I'm going to tell you how it is. First of all, everybody has a soul. You have a soul, and I have a soul. This is a simple fact. Second, babies have souls when they're born, and I know this from Michael and also from being around other babies. Otherwise, they would be little machines or like plants or something. Okay, if babies have souls when they're born, they must also have them before they're born, right? So where does it come from, then? You don't know. But it's there, and it doesn't just go away when someone has a miscarriage."

Then she stopped and we looked at each other for a second. She said, "If you'll think about this, it's common sense."

I started to care again and considered whether I wanted to argue. Usually I don't go in for arguing when the outcome of the argument is irrelevant. This did seem irrelevant, because soul or no soul, Mary and I did not have the baby. It wasn't something that needed discussing. But at the same time, I wanted to tell Rhonda my opinion, since she had been forthcoming with hers, which moreover had not been invited. So I told her, "I do not think that what you said is common sense."

"If so then I am sorry for you," she said.

That made me laugh because of what I was thinking earlier, about wanting her to feel sorry for me. I said, "That's all I really wanted, Rhonda."

Judging from the look on her face, she felt my sarcastic tone to be out of line. I couldn't see how it was even possible for me to be out of line, since I was the childless one and presumably the one whose feelings must be handled with some gentleness here.

Then Rhonda stood up and said she thought we had better drop the subject. She left the kitchen. I finished my coffee and then I went back to bed.

15

WHEN I GOT UP THE SECOND TIME I found Dove in the kitchen at the table, looking just like the standard Dove I was used to. Jimbo had called from the car dealership and Rhonda had gone to get him. "Boy, are you in for a treat," Dove said.

Shortly they arrived with a bag of Hardee's biscuits which Jimbo set down in the middle of the kitchen table. "It was a long night, but I made my point," he said reflectively to the room. Then he noticed me standing by the sink and said, "Hey there skinny, grab you two or three of those biscuits and throw down."

I'm not especially skinny. To put his remark in context, Jimbo himself weighed in the neighborhood of 280 pounds. His height was around six feet, slightly less than mine. He wore a big gray business suit with black specks in it, a powder-blue shirt, and the remains of a silver necktie. The tie was cut off at about the third-button level, apparently with scissors.

He raised both arms over his head, saying, "I prevail!"

Dove gazed quietly into his coffee.

I asked Jimbo, "So you got it all worked out?"

"Yes. All ties are severed with Metropolitan Motors."

"I guess that explains that," I said, indicating his necktie.

"What?" He looked down at his shirt and picked a piece of biscuit off of it. He ate the crumb.

Dove shook his head sadly.

Jimbo was garrulous. My first thought was that the excitement of his nightlong protest had made him talkative, but further experience showed him to be always this way. He liked to roll his shoulders while he talked, as though to keep himself limber, always ready to take a swing at someone or just the air. I would not have bought any kind of car from him. I tried to reserve judgment, though, since I know from the past that my early impressions of people are usually wrong.

"It was a sit-in," he said. "I can't be fired for a reason that isn't in my contract."

"You can be fired for any reason they want," Dove said.

"Wrong! Because I had a satisfactory evaluation. 'Explain that,' I said. 'Explain to me how an employee of this business could get an evaluation marked satisfactory, and then one week later he's fired.' They couldn't explain it. They were speechless. They had no idea of the tussle that was coming. I said, 'You've heard of the civil rights movement? This is the Jimbo MacPherson movement. And I am not moving.'"

He had a biscuit in one hand, and he was trying to pry his shoe off using the other foot without sitting. The shoe wouldn't come off, so he sat down and untied it with his free hand, and then he untied the other. He let out a long "Ah." Then he got up and turned on the oven. Then he sat back down and peeled off his black socks and shed his suit coat onto the back of the chair. He was not a flabby big man. I would describe him as brawny. His hair was brown and lank, and thin on top.

He rubbed his fingertips together to knock the crumbs off, then reached into the bag and grabbed another biscuit. He turned the bag so the open end faced me. To be polite, I ate one. Also I was hungry.

"Life's long and complicated," Jimbo said.

I asked Dove and Jimbo if they smelled anything funny.

"Yes," Dove said.

There was a smell from Jimbo's sit-in socks, but there was also an acrid smell as of leaf smoke. I said, "Is something burning?"

"Yes," Dove said.

Jimbo got an oven mitt and pulled a cookie sheet out of the oven. It appeared from where I stood to have little rocks on it.

"Are those rocks?" I said.

Dove pushed his chair back then and said, "Hold it! Let me leave first." He put a new cigarette in his mouth and left the kitchen.

Jimbo asked me, "Are you into arrowheads?"

I told him I had found something once at a creek by our house that I thought might possibly be an arrowhead. I had since misplaced it.

"Well check out these arrowheads," he said, holding out the cookie sheet.

I went closer and studied them. They were definitely made from something like flint. They were different sizes and shapes, but all were more or less pointed.

"Why are you baking them?"

"I'm seasoning them," he said. "Hey, are we friends?"

"I ate one of your biscuits," I said.

"There's a patina that shows if the arrowhead is old or not. See, I made these arrowheads, Wendell. Would you believe that?"

"I would never have guessed it," I told him.

He explained the process. First he knapped his arrowheads

out of the flintlike stone. Then he put them on the ground on some dirt and sprinkled them with Miracle-Gro and urinated on them every morning. Or depending on his work schedule, which was now up in the air, he could urinate on them at whatever time he got up. He did this for one week, or sometimes two weeks, and then he laid them out on a cookie sheet with none touching and baked them at a low temperature for many hours. The result of this process, which he'd come up with himself, was a simulated old-arrowhead patina. Jimbo claimed he sold the arrowheads to collectors at arrowhead fairs. Then he winked and told me that he never made false claims about his arrowheads, but only said that he'd found them in a cache in the woods behind his house. That was true, because after he baked them he took and left them in the woods awhile. He carried them to the fairs in Ziploc bags. He mentioned that he was part Cherokee.

"So am I," I said.

This stopped him for a moment. I think he thought I was making fun of him. The truth is that I was on the very cusp edge of making fun of him. I am part Cherokee, though. A small part.

I asked him how much he got for his arrowheads.

"It varies a lot," he said.

Dove walked in and said, "Bullshit."

"What's bullshit?"

"Whatever you was saying."

"Oh," Jimbo said. "I get it."

Dove asked Jimbo if he wasn't tired after sitting in all night at the dealership. Jimbo went off on a big talk about how much sleep he needed. "Very little" was the gist of it. He turned his arrowheads one by one with his fingers, interrupting himself sometimes to say "Ouch."

From the back of the house Michael gave a yelp. Nothing awful—he was getting in the tub maybe, I guessed. Rhonda was back there.

I said, "Well, Dove, when do you want to unload that sofa bed?" I had looked it over when I was outside, and the vinyl was sticky from the humid air.

"We need to let baby get his rest," Dove said.

Jimbo said, "Maybe I will." He set the cookie sheet back in the oven and then stood blinking his eyes. Then he walked out of the kitchen.

I looked at Dove and he said quietly, "Wendell, right there went the most worthless son of a bitch I ever knowed. My daughter married him."

"I don't like to talk about him in his own house," I said.

"You're a gentleman."

I heard a rapid thumping noise. Michael came busting into the kitchen naked and opened the refrigerator door. He got out a pack of pudding and tore the lid off. His mother hollered from the back of the house. Michael set the pudding pack on the table next to Dove and ran out of the kitchen again.

Dove was not happy. I sat awhile at the table with him, and we listened to Rhonda and Michael disputing about something at the back of the house. Jimbo yelled once, and then we heard him snoring from the couch in the living room. After a few minutes Dove got up and used a paper towel to pick up Jimbo's socks and drop them in the wastebasket under the sink. I put Michael's pudding back in the refrigerator.

16

I NEEDED A SHOWER, so I took one, carefully, and then I went for a walk up the road and got sweaty again. It was so hot outside the asphalt glistened. I walked as far as the school bus that had been converted to a house. There were flowered curtains in certain windows, and others were sealed with plywood. The exterior of the bus was still its original yellow, with the bus number intact, though the name of the school district was blacked out. The yard of the school-bus home was nicely kept up, except for a circle of orange dust where a Chow dog was kept on a chain. The Chow barked at me. Also there were four or five newly built doghouses on display with for-sale signs. They looked to be good solid dog houses.

I was inspired by the sight of this homestead. Living in a school bus is not for me because it doesn't seem sanitary, but I admired the initiative of someone who would spot the bus at a public auction and say to himself, or to whomever he was going to be living with, "This can be our home." If you go to Home Depot or Lowe's and tell them you're looking for a screen door for your adapted residential school bus they aren't going to be very helpful, because today's building materials are all designed according to a standard system, where every counter is thirty-six inches high and houses are built of studs spaced sixteen or twenty-four inches on center. This allows for quick and convenient construction, but it doesn't touch the pioneer spirit of the person who would build or modify his own house according to his view of how it should be. For me this had been a fond ambition since the time I was little and playing with my Lincoln Logs, though it occurs to me now that Lincoln Logs were also standardized, with their uniform lengths and matching notches. This was part of their appeal.

I don't know what to make of that, but getting back to the point, as I studied this school-bus house I had a renewed hope that I would go home to Tennessee and plunge back into the project of our house with a new vigor. Maybe this time I would not let things like beer and my moods get in the way of fixing the place up so that the house matched the picture of it that I had in my head. This was my dream. Maybe it wasn't the grandest dream, and maybe it even wasn't intelligent, and maybe if I'd had my adulthood to do over again I would have stayed in college as everyone instructed me to, including every member of my family and all of my friends, except one who dropped out at the same time I did and was now captain of a rich widow's yacht in the Bahamas. But I didn't have it all to do over again, and anyway such thoughts are idle and counter to the pioneer spirit I was trying to live by, the essence of which is to look around oneself and say, Here is what I've got, now what can I do with it?

I stood contemplating the bus until a flowered curtain was pulled aside and a man put his head out the window and yelled "Hey!" at me. I waved and left.

Back at Rhonda's house, I watched Jimbo eat half a jar of peanut butter with his finger. He had changed clothes and was now in jeans and a faded red T-shirt. He and Dove and I went out front and looked at the sofa bed in the truck, and Jimbo debated with himself about where in the house it would go. "Maybe in the kitchen," he said. "I like to do things differently from everybody else." This wasn't pioneer spirit but just waywardness. Then Jimbo consulted Rhonda, and then he disagreed with her, and then he asked Dove how much he had originally paid for the sofa. Dove said, "To hell with the whole thing."

"You don't have to be hateful about it," Jimbo said.

Dove pulled out a cigarette and lit the wrong end, or tried to.

"You hateful old man," Jimbo said.

"Kiss my ass," Dove said. He pinched the singed filter off of his cigarette and flicked it away into the yard.

Jimbo went into the house.

"I'm not comfortable here," I said to Dove.

Dove took hold of the banister and eased himself down onto the front-porch steps. "I'm ready to go in a minute," he said. "Let me get this thing smoked." He lit it from the end where the filter had been and took a deep draw.

"Don't let me rush you," I said.

"Why would I want to linger here? I'm not helping anybody."

We sat awhile. He started in on what a bad father he had been, when Rhonda was small. "I loved to drink," he said. "I loved it just as much then as I did now. I mean, as I *do* now."

"Yep."

"I was bad," he said. "I let people down." He turned and looked hard at me. "I'm confiding in you."

Not really, I thought. I had always guessed as much.

"I don't know," he said. "Sometimes I think, a person like me can't do no good and shouldn't try. I've pursued my own interests. I've never give a damn about nothing. Look at this shit hole." He gestured with his hand at the porch and the yard, with Rhonda's Mustang parked in it, about a '91 model, red, with the 5.0-liter engine and the plastic shattered off of one end of the front bumper. "It's her own fault for connecting up with Pea Brain, but it's my fault for how I raised her. I made her expectations low."

He was quiet, and then he clamped his cigarette between his lips and raised up his right arm and gave himself a hard punch in the hip. He grabbed the spot and moaned.

"Take it easy," I said.

He rocked awhile. I couldn't think of anything helpful to say.

When he was still again he said quietly, "I'd like to do her good in some way, but I don't know where to start, besides murdering Jimbo."

"That's about all I can see for him," I said. I was being facetious, and I assumed that Dove also was.

Then Jimbo himself came out the front door. He picked his way down the steps between us and walked across the yard and the road and into Gene's bar. There was one car over there, a brown Lincoln parked near the building. The time was approximately noon.

"Gone to drink his troubles away," Dove said.

"I would never do that myself," I said.

"There's beer in the fridge."

"I thought we drank it all last night."

"While you slept, I did something useful."

I hopped up and was back in a flash with two cold brown uncapped bottles. Already I felt renovated, even before the first sip.

We talked about the heat. We were in shade, where it was bearable, but in another hour it would not be bearable for

Dove. The only air-conditioning in the house was a window unit in the master bedroom.

I told Dove, "I don't know if old Jimbo's so bad. He's just a big loudmouth."

"I know things about him you don't, like his criminal background."

I shrugged.

"I'd kill him myself, if it wasn't immoral," Dove said.

"Well, yes, it's immoral to kill people," I said.

"I know it. Believe me, I thought it through."

"It didn't take a hell of a lot of thinking, I hope."

He looked at me closely and narrowed his eyes. "I come this close to killing him," he said. He held his thumb and finger apart to show me—about a centimeter.

"When did you come that close?"

I got the feeling he was trying to decide how much he wanted to tell me, or how much I was up to hearing.

I said, "Why are we here, Dove?"

He shook his head. "You don't want to know why we're here."

We sat and I considered. By nature I'm a credulous person, if that means it's my impulse to believe what I'm told. Sometimes this causes people to conclude that I'm not as smart as I really am. Perhaps they're right—I am not as smart as I am, sometimes. But I catch up eventually. I said, "What was in the horse trailer, Dove?"

"You should know, you loaded it."

"What was in the boxes at the front?"

"Stuff you needn't worry about."

"Was it something illegal? Was it moonshine?" I knew Dove had a connection to a distributor.

"No, honey," he said.

"Was it something stolen?"

He rolled his head, not shaking it no and not nodding it yes. He said, "Never you mind, honeybunch." He made a dolphin mouth to take a sip of his beer.

"Don't call me honeybunch," I said.

He flipped me the bird.

I told him that I would appreciate being clued in on his illegal activities beforehand, especially when they were scheduled to take place right in front of me. For example, if I had happened on Monday night at the Scotty Inn of Chattanooga to have walked out into the parking lot when somebody was unhooking the trailer from our truck, I might have decided to go cowboy on them.

"Any trouble you started with them boys would have been brought to an abrupt end," he said.

"What are they, organized crime?"

"No, just ordinary ignorant hillbillies," he said. "The dirty fighting kind."

The more I thought, the more angry I was. Some loose ends were getting connected in my mind. I asked him if Walter Furlong had something to do with it.

"I ain't going to talk about what anybody else may have done," Dove said. "That's not the way to be, Wendell."

"You shut up about the way to be," I said.

He raised his big eyebrows and then he laughed.

I got up and went into the house.

17

I GOT A BEER out of the refrigerator and went back to the porch.

"Don't be mad with me, Wendell," Dove said.

"What was it, guns?" I'd heard Dove speak of a flea market in Hillsville, Virginia where unregistered guns were traded.

"No, it wasn't guns," Dove said. "If you must know it was four video-blackjack machines. Perfectly harmless."

"I don't believe you," I said.

"I don't give a whang dang doodle what you believe. It's the truth."

"Is it true?"

"I said it is."

"Where did you get four video-blackjack machines?"

"From an Indian."

"An Indian Indian or a Native American?"

"A Cherokee Indian from North Carolina."

"Well where are they going?"

"To the basement of an AMVETS post."

"Where at?"

"Somewheres in Georgia."

"Then why did you have me put the chairs in there? What was that for, if they were taking the whole trailer?"

"I was done with them chairs. The vinyl was all stained and dull on them."

"What's my cut, then?" I said.

"Oh, foot," he said. He leaned over sideways and worked his hand into his front jeans pocket to reach a roll of bills. He pulled off four fifties and held them out to me.

"This ain't no big-money racket," he said.

I looked at the fifties and at his long, big-knuckled fingers. "Okay, I believe you," I said.

"Congratulations. Take your damn money."

"I don't want it," I said.

"Take it!"

"That would make me an accessory."

"Oh. Well let's not have you be an accessory," he said. He cocked himself sideways to return the roll to his jeans pocket, but then he said, "Oh shit, that pocket's too much trouble." He tucked the money in the pocket of his shirt behind his cigarettes and inhaler.

It was a small concrete porch with a narrow iron rail around it. I went to lean against the rail at the side, and it gave way. I fell two feet into the overgrown, cobwebby azalea bushes. I wasn't hurt, but I was not helped any. I climbed back onto the porch, deliberately leaving the rail askew so that no one else would assume, as I had, that it was solidly mounted.

Dove pulled himself to his feet and said, "I'm going across the road, Wendell."

"I thought we were about to leave."

"Soon as I go over here and have a word with Whosit."

He limped along the concrete path to where it stopped in the middle of the yard alongside the front of Rhonda's Mustang. He steadied himself at the car then carefully ventured onto the sandy gray ground past the walkway. The grass there was snuffed out from being parked on.

"Let's let it rest," I said to Dove.

He stopped in the middle of the road, in the full sun. He apparently wasn't listening to me but catching his breath, because after a moment he moved on. I decided I might as well follow him.

Gene's was the most well-lit bar I have been in. It was one large room with no ceiling. Fluorescent lights were affixed to the roof trusses. Possibly there had been a suspended ceiling at one time. Around the walls were booths that I am guessing came out of an Arby's or Burger King, because the seats were of a bright orange laminate material. The floor was covered in dull red linoleum squares, and at the head of the room there was a long stainless-steel cooler, chest-style, and then a bar made of varnished plywood. Behind the bar, the first thing I noted was a blackjack hanging from a nail. There was also a small color television, which was on, and a big white-haired man in overalls, watching the television.

Dove and I joined Jimbo at a booth. There were two empty Miller Lite bottles on the table, and Jimbo held a third bottle against his chest.

"I'm bored," Jimbo said.

Dove said, "I want to hear what your plans are, Jimbo."

Jimbo looked at me with his eyelids low. Then he twitched his head to give Dove the same look.

I had a thought that I guess I have had before, which is that being physically large gives a person the same kind of self-assurance that being wealthy seems to give. Whether you can whip any man in the room or pay to have him whipped, it amounts to the same.

"My plans," Jimbo said. "I'm thinking I'd like to get out of sales for a while."

"Oh, you're out of sales. What I want to know is how you intend to pay rent and feed my daughter and grandson, now that you had her quit her job."

"I didn't have her quit her job. She didn't like her job, and she wanted to quit it."

"Nobody likes their job."

"She wants to be home with Michael," Jimbo said. He drained his beer and slid himself out of the booth.

"Somebody has to work," Dove said.

Jimbo brought three bottles from the cooler and sat back down. He said he would have expected Dove to be glad for his daughter, that she was back with her husband as a family, working out differences. He said it was important that he was being a hands-on father now, involved in his child's rearing.

"Don't take a lofty tone with me, asshole," Dove said.

Jimbo sighed and sat very still.

"I won't be preached to by an ex-convict," Dove said. "I won't sit through that bullshit. You don't know how close you come to dying today. If it wasn't for Rhonda and Michael, I'd have shot you. How I'd have loved that."

"Settle down," Jimbo said, smirking.

Dove roared. "Oh shit!" he yelled. "Do not tell me to settle! Come over here!" Dove half stood up, as well as he could in the booth, and at the same time reached out both arms for Jimbo's face. Jimbo grabbed Dove's wrist and wouldn't drop it. Dove made a face like a chimp, trying to peel Jimbo's cigarlike fingers away.

The white-haired man behind the bar spoke. "No fighting," he said.

Dove was shouting in open-exhaust mode. He swung his

free hand towards Jimbo's face again, with his fingers bent, clawing at Jimbo's eyes. Jimbo knocked his arm away.

I grabbed Jimbo's arm and tried to open his hand, the one clamped on Dove's wrist. His hand was as hard as a potato.

"No fighting," the man said from behind the bar.

Then Jimbo decided to let go of Dove's wrist. Dove shoved me in the ribs, because I was on the outside of the booth seat, blocking him in. I yelped and scooted out of his way. Dove struggled up out of the seat and moved like a hurt spider across the red tile and out the door.

"Stop smiling," I said to Jimbo.

"Sit down," he said.

I said, "I don't go in for pushing old men around."

"He started it."

"I don't care. You could be more respectful towards him."

"Oh, he's all right. Look at him move."

I looked out the window where Jimbo pointed. Dove was scooting across the road at the quickest pace I had ever seen him go. He rocked side to side and held his arms out for balance.

I rubbed my side where Dove had jabbed me.

Jimbo twisted the caps off of two of the beers. "You don't know the other side of the story, Wendell," he said. "All I get from the man is verbal abuse. It's unceasing."

I sat down. I said, "Look at it this way. He's old and sick. He could die soon. He doesn't like you, but it's because he's concerned for his daughter and Michael. You can understand his way of looking at this."

"The man just now said he wanted to shoot me, Wendell. Has anybody ever said that to you?"

"Not recently." I took a quick sip from the beer.

"Well, conjure on that awhile, my friend. You know he went to prison for shooting a man."

I knew Dove had been in prison, but I had never heard what for.

"He'll tell you it was self-defense, of course. But the thing is, what were the events that led up to him needing to defend himself in that way?"

"This is too much for me to think about," I said. "I just want to unload the damned couch and go home."

"That couch is ugly. I don't want the couch."

I asked him what he had been in jail for.

"A burned-out taillight, plus one bale of cannabis in the trunk. You're married, right?"

"Yes."

"You got kids?"

"No."

"Have kids," he said. "It gives meaning to existence."

"That's a hell of a thing to say."

"It's what I believe. Look at the craziness, Wendell. I don't have a job today. What about that? A ninety-year-old man wants to kill me."

"He's sixty-nine," I said.

"Not Dove. I'm talking about my asshole ex-boss that fired me. What am I going to do now?"

"I don't know."

"If you have a criminal record it's damned hard to get a job in this economy."

"I don't know what to tell you, Jimbo."

He turned up his bottle and sucked all twelve ounces down in several gulps. He wiped his chin and asked me if I wanted to split the last beer.

"How's that going to work?" I said. "Is there a glass?"

"I don't know. Gene, have you got a glass?"

Gene ducked under the plywood bar and shortly he came up with a plastic cup. He brought it over.

"Gene, this is Wendell," Jimbo said.

"Hi, Gene," I said.

"Hi, Wendell. I'm glad to meet you." He smiled a pleasant smile, and we shook hands. "You need to give some thought to the company you're keeping," he said.

"We all do," Jimbo said.

18

AFTER THE BEER I left Jimbo to ponder his existence and went back across the street to check on Dove. Rhonda was using her Ellender lung power on him. Between the two of them, they had enough breath to inflate a truck tire. "You don't listen to reason!" Dove yelled.

Rhonda lit into him:

"You mean I don't listen to you! Because you've got no place to tell us how to live! Anything Jimbo ever did wrong, you did it twice, and couldn't even be bothered to lie about it! And you're cruel. You're the nerviest bastard I ever heard of!"

"I want to help you!" Dove said. "I'm trying to help and make up for things!"

I backed out the door at this point and into the front yard. I thought I'd wander off for a while. I walked to the end of the house and around the corner. There was a narrow side yard bordered with trees and brush. The backyard was impassable, blocked up by various clutter including a disassembled swing set and a massive brick barbecue grill. I heard something rustle and looked behind me into the trees, and there was Michael. His body faced the woods, but he was looking at me over his shoulder. I said, "Michael, are you all right, buddy? They're hashing things out. They're not hurting each other."

He stepped away from me slowly, still looking back.

I said, "What are you doing, bud?"

"Peeing," he said.

I turned away. I said, "Have you got some of Jimbo's arrowheads down there?"

I heard no answer so I looked again. He shook his head no.

Then it occurred to me, maybe that whole business about urinating on the arrowheads was just Jimbo pulling my leg. But the cookie sheet was a fact. I had seen it.

Michael and I wandered back into the woods. It was cooler there, though still hot. The ground was covered with long red pine needles. When I say long I mean fifteen inches, much longer than any pine needle I was used to seeing in East Tennessee. I picked a few up to examine and noticed that they all came in clusters of three. The smell was rich and rosiny.

Michael moved around a lot. He didn't simply walk in a line. He would trot up ahead to something and fiddle with it, like a fallen trunk with pads of moss on it, and then run off sideways and pull a root up, and then run back to me, burning a lot of energy as I guess children usually do, or dogs for that matter. I asked him if he had any friends in the neighborhood, and he told me I believe the name of every friend he had ever known in his life that he could remember, although it was unclear to me whether any of them lived nearby. Then I asked him about school, and whether he was happy to be going back in September, and he said he didn't know. We found some standing water and he got his shoes wet, and then he began collecting things from the ground and off plants, telling me which ones I could eat if I was hungry and which ones I couldn't. I supposed this was some

bullshit he had picked up from Jimbo, and I hoped Michael
didn't really believe it, because he was telling me to eat bark
off of a pine tree, which I don't believe is actually done. I told
him not to eat bark. I said, "I hope you don't ever get stuck in
the woods, Michael."

"It could happen," he said.

I said, "Are you afraid of snakes?"

"No."

"Do you kill them when you see them?"

He looked worried a bit, and then he said, "No."

I said, "Very slowly, then, look right here, and here is a
snake." I pointed, and he looked and saw it. It was a regular
black snake.

He asked me to pick it up.

"I don't go in for picking up snakes," I said.

We watched it awhile, with me holding Michael back, but
he wouldn't stop fidgeting, and the snake left. I said, "My wife
is a big fan of snakes. If she had been here she would have
picked it up."

He said, "I have a friend named Louise, and her mother
bought some lotion for her knees."

"What's wrong with them? Are her knees chapped?"

"I don't know," Michael said.

We wandered back towards the yard, and I heard Dove's
truck roar to life. It made quite an announcement on starting.
Michael and I went to the front of the house, and Dove was at
the wheel. He waved us over and said to me, "Are you coming
or staying?"

I went up to where Michael couldn't hear us and said, "Well
I'm not staying."

"Come on then."

I told him to wait while I put Michael in the house. Then I

looked and I couldn't find Michael, until I realized he was standing by my legs. I said, "I'm going to pick you up, okay?"

He nodded.

I picked him up. He was simply a small person, and to lift him was satisfying. It was not something I had ever done much of, not being from a big family or having much cause to lift children. I was a little clumsy with him until I found a way to get him on my shoulder, and then he rode all right. At the door I put him down and made him take his wet shoes off, and then I heaved him to my shoulder again and ducked through the doorway.

I was headed to the kitchen but saw through the kitchen door that Rhonda had her head down on the table. I plopped Michael onto the sofa in the living room.

He lay on his back and stared at me. I asked him if I had hurt him. He said "No."

I went to the kitchen doorway. I said, "Rhonda, I'm heading out with Dove. Michael's in here on the couch."

She sat up, her back to me, and turned halfway so I saw her in profile. "Thanks Wendell," she said.

"Okay. Thanks Rhonda," I said.

She put her head down again.

I got sad. I was sad for Mary, though—not for Rhonda or Michael or Dove or even myself. I thought, Please let Mary be happy somehow.

Then I went back and gave Michael a jostle and told him to give me a call sometime and we could meet for breakfast. He squinted at me and said, "I don't know your phone number," so I pulled out my wallet and gave him my last business card. Then I left.

19

DOVE AND I DROVE OUT a different way than we had come in, not on purpose but because Dove wasn't paying attention, because he was upset. We wound up lost, but Dove didn't want to turn around and go back past Rhonda's house.

We came to a Conoco station with a store in it and got beer and snack food and directions to town. I got behind the wheel and we sat and drank a couple of beers in the parking lot of the Conoco. It was midafternoon now, and the black-vinyl-covered padding along the top of the dashboard was too hot to touch. I said to Dove, "Michael's a perfect little kid. I just like the hell out of him."

Dove said nothing, so I said, "Let's go back and get him and take him with us."

Dove said, "I heard of a word for that, Wendell, and it's called kidnapping somebody."

"Hell," I said, and I meant to say more. But what?

We got on our way. We came to a drive-in movie theater called the Beverly Drive-In, which was one of the landmarks we had been told at the Conoco we couldn't miss because it was painted dinner-mint green, and it was. We turned right onto

Highway 49, and that took us north into town and then on to
what appeared to be the main drag of Hattiesburg, Mississippi.
It was the same road we had been on coming into town, but a
different section. I almost rear-ended a Subaru Outback at a
stoplight because I was watching two kids kissing on the sidewalk in front of a drugstore. They were quite at their ease and
to make it even more unusual, the girl was taller than the boy
and she was running her hands all over her own head while he
was kissing her. Dove had not noticed them and so fortunately
was looking ahead, and he hollered and I slammed the brakes
on and everybody was all right. Then I pointed the kissers out
to Dove, and he leaned out his window and bayed at them.

We found a motel called Family Lodge, and Dove went in to
pay. I let him, since he had the fat bankroll. When we got to
the room I said, "It's time I had some toiletries of my own,
Dove." He had been letting me borrow his deodorant, but that
gets old, and also I wanted a razor because I had not shaved
since Friday morning, and it was Wednesday. Lending razors is
a bit too intimate. Dove said, "Okay bye," and he gave me a key
card to the room then went into the bathroom and shut the
door.

I started to get myself another beer to take with me, but
then I thought, No, I'm driving in a strange town, and it
wouldn't be wise. So I finished the one I had open and went out
without one. When I got in the truck I asked myself, Should I
make a new rule not to ever drive when I'm drinking? Everyone knows it's not good. But on the other hand, how would I
get places if I didn't drive? I was conjuring on this when I
backed the truck out of the parking spot and damn if I didn't
nearly back it into a new Dodge Ram dually pickup, a big
freaking gaudy mess with a crew cab and the Cummins turbo
diesel engine, which has a sound reminding me of the Metro-

politan Atlanta Rapid Transit Authority. The truck was black, and the man driving it had on a large ridiculous felt cowboy hat with feathers hanging off of it, and more feathers dangled from the rearview mirror. I noticed the inside decor when the man stopped to power down his window so I could see him throw me the bird.

I slung Dove's truck into drive, and it lurched back into the parking space out of the big Dodge's way. But then I missed the brake pedal, and the Ford rolled up onto the parking stop and popped the front right tire.

Hellfire! I got out of the truck and looked at what I had done. There was an inch of rebar sticking up past the top of the concrete stop. This had punctured the tire. I went back to the truck bed to locate the spare, which I was glad to see had air in it, but I was sorry to see it was wedged between the front of the truck bed and the sofa.

I went to the cab at the passenger side and pushed the seat forward to find the jack. Back there I found beer cans, soup cans, pieces of thermal clothing, a length of green hose, a *Hustler* that had been rained on, and other bits of trash, all of it dusty, and under the dust, greasy. It was about as bad a behind-the-seat area as I have seen, and it surprised me since Dove's house was a scrupulously clean bachelor dwelling. Everyone has things about them you don't expect. I dug in and found the jack and lug wrench and extricated them from some badly tangled jumper leads, and then I was done behind the seat. I stood up quick and whop, I banged the backside of my head on the edge of the truck roof. I banged it but good, and I crumpled and sat down in the parking lot there on a spot of spilled Coca-Cola, helpless. I may have blacked out briefly.

In a moment I tried to stand. I didn't want somebody spotting me there and calling an ambulance. I pulled myself up by the door handle, and then the door swung open and I fell down again. Then I got up successfully and was dizzy and in some pain, but standing. I thought I had better settle down some before attempting to raise the truck, so I found the key card for the room, in my pocket, and then remembered to shut the truck door, and then went into the room to lie down.

I heard water running in the bathroom. Dove's bag was open on the bed, and some things were pulled out of it. I sat down on the other bed, and then I touched my head and got up to look in the mirror over the sink, to see if I was bleeding. On the mirror I discovered a note that had been stuck to the glass with a great deal of soap and water. It was on motel notepaper. The handwriting was not the best, but I made out the following:

Don the sofa is yours. Go home to Mary and I hope she takes you back. Dove.

I didn't understand this. Below was another line that said,

Do not infer the bathroom.

This made even less sense to me. Dove was in the bathroom, and I wanted in there when he got out.

I looked at my head, but because of the location of where I had hit it, I could not directly see the knot. The word "infer" was not one that I had need of very often, but even dazed I was fairly certain that the word was not being used right in that sentence. I said loudly, so he could hear me over the running water, "Dove, what do you mean, 'Do not infer the bathroom'?"

He didn't answer. I stood for some time thinking nothing, and then I looked at the note on the mirror again and saw "enter," not "infer."

I opened the bathroom door and went in. Dove was sitting up in the bathtub and there was steam everywhere, and I saw that in his hand on the edge of the tub he held a gun.

"Give me that," I said.

He looked at me. His eyes were red, and he made a huffling, choking sound. He didn't move.

I knelt and grabbed his arm, and he grabbed onto the gun with his other hand. We both pulled until I got a good enough hold to twist the gun out of his grip. I got up and walked out of the bathroom.

I'm no gun expert. This was a short-barreled revolver of a large caliber. I took the bullets out and put them in my pocket, and then I carried the gun back into the bathroom with the cylinder hanging out and shook it at him. "What in the hell are you doing with this damn gun in the bathtub?" I said.

Dove was coughing and heaving, clutching at the side of the tub, and then he sat up straight and got a breath and yelled at me to get out and shut the door.

"I'm not getting out until you tell me what you're doing with the damn gun inside the bathroom!"

"What do you think?"

He twisted, and water splashed over the tub wall onto the floor.

"Turn off the water!" I said.

"Go away!"

I reached in and shut the water off myself. Then I left and shut the door and went to his bag on the bed. I searched through it quickly and found a plastic bag with more bullets in it. I put these in my pocket too.

I beat the gun on the nightstand, trying to knock the cylinder off or something, but all I was doing was gouging the edge of the nightstand. I went over to the door and smacked the gun one time against the heavy steel doorknob. I went back into the bathroom. I said, "Shit, Dove!"

He was still in the tub, leaning sideways against the tiled wall. He moved his head enough to look at me, then looked down.

"I wasn't going to do it," he said.

"Bullshit!"

"Easy," he said. "Take it easy, please, Wendell."

"I won't take it easy!" I said. My head throbbed, and I walked out and circled in the room and then came back to the bathroom and sat down on the floor with my back against the door frame. "I'm not up to this," I said.

A minute passed. The air was moist. I had to catch my breath. Dove said, "Give me some paper, Wendell." I was confused until I saw he meant paper to blow his nose with. I tore some off the roll and gave it to him.

"I was only trying it out," he said.

I set the gun down on the tile between my feet.

"I don't know whether I could do it or not," he said. "I scared myself."

"Just leave me out of it in the future," I said.

"I didn't invite you in here, asshole."

"You're the asshole," I said.

"I come closer to breaking my neck getting in this tub than I did shooting myself."

He asked me to go get the bottle of Henry McKenna out of his bag. I did it, and I poured us each a shot in a plastic Family Lodge cup.

"You're shaking, Wendell," he said.

"I'm all right."

He reached for the gun on the floor and I kicked it back towards myself so he couldn't reach it. Then I leaned over and shut the shower curtain, so I wouldn't have to look at him.

"That gun needs to be dried off," he said.

"Let me worry about it," I said. "I want you to tell me something. Jimbo says you shot somebody."

"When?"

"I don't know when. You tell me when."

"I've been shot at more times than I've shot at someone."

"Were you going to shoot Jimbo when we came here?"

"Hell, I don't know, Wendell. Yes, I was. That was my intention."

"Why?"

"If you don't already see that, I can't explain it to you."

"That's the wrong way to think," I said. "There's something wrong with a person who would even consider shooting his son-in-law."

"Different people handle things different ways, Wendell."

I got a refill on my drink and took a sip. With my free hand I pressed down on the top of my head, which helped the headache.

"I'm bad," Dove said.

I told him I had popped a tire on his truck.

"That's a pisser," he said.

"Your sofa is blocking the spare," I said. "I don't see why you brought the sofa, if the point of the trip was killing Jimbo."

"That sofa has thirty-eight thousand cash in it."

"Dollars?"

"Yes, dollars. Down beside the cushion."

I asked him why he would put thirty-eight thousand dollars in cash down beside the cushion of a convertible sofa in the back of his truck.

"The sofa wasn't in the truck when I put the money there," he said. "I chose to leave it there so it wouldn't get stole."

I reached up the wall behind me and hit the switch that turned off the light and the exhaust fan in the ceiling. I had not realized it until then, but the rattling of the fan had been bugging the living hell out of me. "There is such a thing as a savings bank," I said.

He asked me if I was stupid.

"Yes. You have to explain everything very slow to me," I said.

"After I shot Jimbo, I was counting on going to prison. They ain't got banks in prison, Wendell, nor ATM machines neither."

"Will they let you carry a sofa in with you?"

"Look, I never had all the details figured out, all right? But now I'm not killing nobody, so I'm not expecting to go to the pen anymore. So forget it, please."

I told him his bourbon would be good if we had some ice to put in it.

"Run get us some, and I'll put on some clothing."

I asked him where he had gotten the thirty-eight thousand dollars.

He pushed the curtain aside to give me a stern look. "Laying block," he said.

"You saved that much?"

"I sold my place."

"You sold your place in Kingsport?"

"How many places do you think I have?"

"Where will you live now?"

"I don't know that. The situation is all-around stupid. I hate to ask you this now, buddy, but I'm not able to get out of this tub by myself."

I swallowed the rest of my drink and helped Dove out of the tub.

"Now you've seen me at my lowest," he said.

"I hope so."

He told me I had a mean side that he had never known about. Then he said he wanted his bullets back.

"Go to hell," I said. I called him a bastard and told him I was almost ready to stop fooling with him. I was drunk.

He got into bed. We had some more drinks, and I turned on a lamp. Dove said, "I might have pulled the trigger, Wendell, except I remembered I hadn't told you about that money in the sofa. You and Mary could use that."

"Mary who?" I said.

"Don't give me that shit. That's not funny at all."

"I don't want your money," I said. "I don't want you to die."

"Everybody dies," he said. "I wish I would go ahead and die."

"No you do not."

"Don't I?"

"No," I said. I could hear my voice getting thick. I was getting that out-of-my-body feeling. It was like I was watching myself with one eye and floating. Dove talked on about how I didn't know what it felt like to be him, and sixty-nine years old, and not able to walk across the room without gasping for breath. "You're young and all your body functions are intact," he said. "You don't know about being old, and can't sleep, and can't pee."

"Well, but you still don't give up," I said.

"Eventually you got to."

"No. Life is good," I said.

"Is it, now?"

"Yes."

"What's so good about it?"

I was trying to clear my head. I told him maybe he could get married again.

"Bring them on," he said. He slapped his leg under the sheet.

"You've got some money," I said.

"Don't forget my truck. She's a classic."

"You have friends," I said. "Some would miss you. Not me, but Walter Furlong would. How would Walter feel if you checked out?"

"Walter wouldn't hold it against me. His old man shot himself."

I was sitting on the bed, weaving. I went to stand up and got dizzy and had to grab some furniture. I worked my way across the room to the sink, to wash my face.

"You're a poor sight," Dove said.

I told Dove I was going to get drunker than I had ever been in my life, and then I would hide his gun somewhere, and when I woke up I would not be able to remember where I had hid it.

Dove said, "You're one of them sons of bitches that hangs on way past time when everybody else sees hope is lost. Aren't you?"

"No," I said.

20

I DROPPED OFF HARD, passed out you might say, at some awful hour and had a dream that was a twisted version of an already twisted movie Dove and I had been watching on Cinemax. It was definitely a sex movie, but it had an artistic slant. For example, some women would be kissing each other and so on and then one of them would stop and give a speech about some encounter she had with a dog trainer in college, and the speech would last for ten minutes while the other woman made a salad in the nude. I found it puzzling, but Dove said he didn't care if the lady hoed corn as long as she had every stitch of her clothes off.

I dreamed about this movie, except in my version we went to the bathtub and found Dove, and I woke up thinking he was dead, then remembering he wasn't. Then I remembered I was in a Family Lodge in Hattiesburg, and felt miserable. And then I remembered that I had punctured the tire on Dove's truck. I was already dressed, so I slipped out to the parking lot to finish changing it, but when I got out there and had a look at the tire, truck, and jack again I decided to wait. It was still dark, and I was still partly drunk. I went looking for the hotel restaurant, never thinking that it wouldn't be open at four in the morning, nor that moreover there wasn't a hotel restaurant at the Family Lodge.

I wound up at the front desk. By the time my eyes adjusted the desk guy had already seen me and he was sitting, it appeared, on a tall stool behind the counter and staring directly at me. He looked about twenty-one. He had a round, messy face and black hair. He wore a white shirt with a motel logo on it and a plastic tag. I said, "Hello."

He didn't say anything. I figured he had already said hello without my hearing.

I said, "Do you mind if I sit down?" He still didn't answer, so I said, "Are you alive?"

He shook his head and said, "Hi."

I sat down on one of the two sofas at the other end of the lobby. It was shadowy in this corner, so I went to switch on a lamp. It wouldn't come on, and on further investigation I found it to not be plugged in to the wall. I reached under the table and plugged it in, and it gave me a shock. I threw the lamp into the other sofa. I had been holding it in my hand so I wouldn't knock it over when I went under the table. It was a tall and skinny chrome lamp.

The kid at the desk was still watching me. I said to him, "Something is wrong with that lamp."

"What?"

I told him it had shocked me, and he came over. The lamp was lit, on its side on the cushion. I got up and moved it back to the table.

"It didn't shock you that time," he said.

"That's because I wasn't touching the receptacle cover that time."

"I don't know what that means," he said.

I told him to reach under the table and touch the receptacle cover on the wall, and then reach and turn the lamp off. He did it and got shocked. In fact, he didn't even get the lamp switched off before it threw him.

"Ouch," he said.

I adjusted the lamp back to where it had been on the table and sat down again.

The boy asked me if I wanted some coffee.

"Who made it?" I said.

He said he'd made it himself, but it was a fairly automatic process involving a premeasured pouch of coffee and a button.

I didn't want to be drunk anymore. The feeling is kind of like the one in a dream where you are trying to walk fast but can't, and can't tell why. The shock had done me some good, and a cup of coffee might help further, I thought. I had one and the boy was right, it tasted like any plain coffee that you would get anywhere in the United States of America, and I drank it while he told me about a band he was in with his girl-friend and her brother. It was difficult for him to be in a band with his girlfriend, he said, because when he played he liked to be professional, and that meant no kissing, cuddling, or other distractions, only work. Some people don't realize the hard work and commitment that are required of a person who wants to make it large in the music industry today, he told me. It takes years of study and preparation, he said.

"Well I'm an electrician, and any dumbass can do that," I said.

He said he had been shocked by a microphone recently and asked could I explain what caused it to happen.

I told him electricity seeks a path to ground. We stared

awhile at nothing, and then I mentioned that I had decided to give up drinking. He said, "Why?"

I said, "I don't like the effect it's having in my life."

He said, "I copy that." He said, "It'll also ruin your health, because it screws your sleep up, and that screws your immune system. I'm all for you renouncing it completely, man."

"That's what I intend."

"Why drink anyway?"

"Because it's fun."

He said, "I like fun. But let me tell you this"—his eyes rolled as he said this, and his gaze seemed to scrape across the edge of the ceiling behind me—"that's not the only way to have fun, and there are safer ways in this day and time."

"Like what?"

"Like I don't know, but I have this friend who knows a lot about it, because he was a nurse in the navy. Today there's pharmaceutical products that do all of the good things for you that alcohol could ever do, with none of the dangerous side effects. I mean the worst thing that might ever happen with some of these drugs is you get a really dry mouth."

"Alcohol does that."

"Well, I hate it. But then you just drink some juice and you're good to go."

The phone rang behind the desk, and he bolted for it in such a hurry that he slipped and fell down on the tile. Still he got to the phone before the fourth ring.

I stretched out on my back. I had a feeling that at that moment it would be possible for me to slip into a beautiful deep sleep from which I would awake rested and whole. But if I got up and walked back to the room, the feeling would be gone by the time I got there, I felt. The kid hung up the phone and said across the lobby, "Sir, don't get the wrong impression that I'm trying to sell you something. First off, you could be a cop for all I know, so I wouldn't offer to sell you anything even if I had it to sell, which I don't."

I said, "I already told you I'm an electrician."

He came back to my side of the lobby and said, "If you're an electrician why did you get shocked by that lamp?"

"Electricians get shocked all the time."

"That's a rough way to live."

I felt sad and nostalgic because I could see that the perfect moment for falling asleep on that sofa had already slipped past.

He said, "I can prove I don't deal. Wait here a minute." He went back into the office and called out again, "Wait just a minute." I shut my eyes and had a feeling of dread. There was a hissing sound suddenly like a broken gas line, and it startled me so that I sat up. It turned out he had put on a tape of his band and it was playing over the speakers in the ceiling. He came back out and said there was no way he could write songs for this band and perform "gigs," as he called them, and also have time to deal. I said, "You're right, that proves it. I don't suspect you."

"What do you think of my band?"

It sounded like somebody mumbling, plus some guitars thumping around, plus some drums. I said, "I can't understand the words."

"That's okay, because the CD will come with a lyric sheet."

I guess he could tell I didn't like it, though, because he went back in the office and turned it off.

When he came back he started in on his songs, and how he wrote them, and how many he could write per week, and whether they were good. He said he hoped they were good, and the way he said it made me like him better than I did before. He said, "I make them as good as I can, and I so, so want them to be good, man." He wanted it so much that it made me want them to be good, too, and I told him I hoped he would get famous so someday I could tell people, "That guy gave me a cup of coffee one time when he was still a nobody."

He said, "Hey, I'm not a nobody."

"Oops, sorry."

"Not according to Mom anyway," he said, and we both had a laugh. Then he went on at great length about how his band's sound should be described, and what their influences were, and what their first CD cover would look like, and how musicians ought to dress. He thought everybody ought to dress himself, and nobody should pay someone else to dress him. I said I could agree with that, although my wife sometimes had something to say about what I put on, but she was not paid to do that but did it free, to help me. He said he had a couple of times tried telling his girlfriend what to wear, and she didn't like it so he stopped. Then he wanted me to pretend I was an interviewer for *Rolling Stone* and ask him some questions, but that seemed a touch fruity to me. I said, "I don't know about that. I have a comfort level." Then an elderly couple came in wanting their continental breakfast. He said, "I'm sorry, folks, but the continental breakfast isn't served until six."

The man said, "What time is it now?"

The desk kid looked at the clock and said, "It's just after five."

The couple looked at me sitting up on the sofa, and then they looked at the kid again, and then they came to the other sofa and sat down to wait.

The lady stared at my shoes, which were a mess. I shut my eyes and when I opened them, she was staring at my face. It was time to go back to the room, so I did.

21

LATER THAT MORNING I let Dove know that I thought we needed to change things and do better. I said, "Lying in the bed drinking liquor and watching Cinemax is no kind of life. I already made up my mind that I'm stopping drinking, and I suggest you do the same."

He was brushing his teeth in his jeans and undershirt, barefooted, and when I said "do the same" he went into baby bird. He grabbed a motel towel and wiped the toothpaste off his mouth, and then he turned around and pointed the toothbrush at me. He said, "Wendell, you'd best give up that shit right now. I've left wives and babies over that kind of talk, and I will damn sure drop your ass by the road, my friend."

He was in absolute earnest. I knew it because a minute later, after he had finished brushing his teeth, he said, "Now Wendell, I didn't mean to get cross with you on that, but I just won't have it. But don't be mad at me, now."

I wasn't mad, but his saying this made me wonder if I ought to be. I said, "I just am ready for something different, is all. I'd like to recover some zest for life."

He considered this thoughtfully, and then he nodded but didn't say anything.

We got cleaned up and were ready to go find some breakfast when I remembered the tire. I changed it, and then we drove up the road to an International House of Pancakes where I ordered a plate of melon parts and cottage cheese. Dove had an omelet.

"Now what?" I said.

"Why don't you go run several miles?"

I suggested to him that we drive down to the coast. I had noticed in some of the brochures in the lobby of the Family Lodge that they had some attractions down there that might beguile us a little, like Marine Life and so on.

He squinted and lit a cigarette, and we sat several minutes without talking. I thought again, and I saw that going to the coast was a stupid idea, and what I needed to do was go home and settle affairs with Mary. I dreaded it. Finally Dove said, "Okay, let's go to the coast, Wendell." He stubbed out his cigarette. I said, "Okay," and we headed out.

It was another glaringly bright and steamy day in Mississippi. To be outside in the air was like having hot, wet pieces of cardboard laid over your face and arms. It was a challenge that I kind of enjoyed for its exoticness, always reminding me that I was in a strange and not completely hospitable place. Dove suffered, though. He turned red, short of breath, and sullen. In the truck he rode quietly with ice cubes bundled in a T-shirt and pressed to his throat.

We took U.S. Highway 49 south. It was a split four-lane, enclosed for long stretches by dense pine woods. A rabbit could have penetrated these woods, but an ordinary dog would have had slow going. The pavement on 49 south of Hattiesburg was of an unusual wrenlike shade of brown that I had never noticed on pavement before. I studied it up close when we stopped at a Chevron for more ice and discovered that it was an asphalt composite containing a high percentage of smooth brown gravels. I liked this South Mississippi light brown road surface.

After an hour on this road the landscape opened out and I began to sense the beach approaching. The parking lots were sandier, and the billboards mentioned water and gambling. Everything else in my life notwithstanding, I was excited about seeing the Gulf of Mexico for the first time.

Dove said, "I'm ready to be in some air-conditioning now, Wendell." I stopped at a place called Taco Sombrero, and he went to a booth and I went to get him some water.

Unusually for a fast-food restaurant, Taco Sombrero sold Budweiser. I took a pass, though it felt strange, like a wasted opportunity. Instead of beer I got a bean burrito.

Dove looked a little better as he cooled off and watched me eat my burrito. I asked him if he wanted to go to Marine Life, and he said he didn't care what we did as long as it was climate-controlled.

"Try to care a little," I said. "It makes it easier to decide what to do next."

"But I don't care what we do next."

"Well, maybe we shouldn't do anything," I said. "I'm content to sit here and eat this burrito. This may be the best burrito I ever ate in my life, Dove."

"I can't eat them things," he said. "Is that just only beans in there?"

"Yes sir."

He shook his head disapprovingly. "I thought I'd done give

up caring about anything, and then I got aggravated enough at my son-in-law that I started caring again. But that was unpleasant, so I plan to not care anymore forever."

"That's the first I've heard you refer to him as your son-in-law," I said.

"I only call him that because I'm sick of hearing a word that starts with 'J' and ends with 'O.'"

"Is it nice, not caring?"

"It's tolerable."

"Maybe I'll not care, too."

He gave a bored sigh. "You got a wife and a home to think of, Wendell."

"They're out of the picture. I'm focused on my burrito now."

He watched my burrito with big toadlike eyes.

With my mouth full, but with my open hand shielding my mouth from his view, I said, "This is a good burrito. This is the only thing I care about."

Dove took his cigarette pack from behind the inhaler in his shirt pocket and shook it. A cigarette flew out and landed on the floor, and a lady in a nurse's uniform who was walking by with a tray of food stepped on the cigarette without noticing. I picked it up off of the floor, I don't know why, just without thinking, and then I held it out to Dove. "I ain't smoking that dirty thing," Dove said.

22

WE RODE ON DOWN 49 INTO GULFPORT and through it, all
the way to where the highway ended in a "T" with U.S. 90.
There we turned eastward. I saw glimpses of the water past
some industrial-type piers and warehouse buildings and then a
marina. Then I had an unobstructed view of white sand and
water. "Look, the gulf," I said to Dove.

"It ain't near as pretty as in Florida," Dove said.

The highway runs along the beach, though sometimes for a
stretch the view is blocked by restaurants, souvenir stores, or a
motel. On the inland side there are commercial stretches, and
then there are some grand residences as well. I would have
been glad to move into one of these mansions that day and call
Mary to join me.

We passed out of Gulfport and into Biloxi. We saw a casino
built to look like a pirate ship. Dove had heard somewhere that
they gave free drinks at the casinos. We passed the pirate ship
but further along stopped at another casino where we discovered they wouldn't give us free drinks unless we were gambling. Dove told the cocktail waitress, who wore a small rigid
dress, that he could get drunk quicker and more economically

at the VFW than standing and feeding quarters into a slot machine for an occasional free beer. "Yes sir, that's right," she said.

I said, "For that matter you could go to the Exxon and get a case to drink in the truck."

"You don't need to be drinking in your truck," the cocktail waitress said.

"There's a sofa in back," I told her. "He can stretch out, and I'll do the driving."

"But the sofa ain't air-conditioned," Dove said.

Did we live somewhere? the woman asked. Her name tag said KELLY. Her breasts roosted in the cups of her dress like small white hens.

"We're from Tennessee," Dove said.

"Do you have a room?"

"No, but that's a good idea. We can get us a room, Wendell."

Kelly told us if we would play just a few quarters she would bring us each one beer, and we could drink it and then go get a room and save our money.

"We've made a friend," Dove said.

Kelly smiled charmingly at that. She brought us two Michelobs, for which I was glad because I don't care for Michelob. Dove gave her the rest of the roll of quarters that he had bought, and we wandered through the casino gawking. It was kind of how I picture hell to be, with big dim rooms and hundreds of people packed in, and they're all working very hard but not getting anything done, and there's a constant racket of dingers going off, and sirens. Dove finished his Michelob slowly and said, "That's a good beer. Maybe I'll switch brands."

I gave him mine, which was unsipped. I said, "Do these people know they're throwing their money away?"

"No skin off your ass."

"I just think it's somewhat alarming, Dove."

"Some people like to be alarmed," he said. Then he gave me a mild lecturing on how I was getting too judgmental lately and I ought to give it a rest because it was irksome to him and also pointless.

"When you tell me not to be judgmental, you are being judgmental," I said.

"My judgment is better than yours because I've been around the block, and I'm not uptight like you are," he said.

"I'm not uptight. I just don't go in for wasting a lot of money that someone earned."

"On the other hand, very few gets paid what they're truly worth," Dove said. "Some are paid more than they're worth, and some are paid less. That's why I don't put a lot of stock in your bullshit about earning your damn money, Wendell."

We weren't making a lot of progress here and I wanted air, so I told Dove I would be waiting outside for him. "You'll be waiting a while," he said.

I went outside to the deck that connected the casino, which was built over water on some kind of a barge, to the parking garage and hotel, on land. The barge was tethered by means of heavy chains to steel pilings so that it could rise and sink with the tide. This setup seemed like a lot of trouble to go to, just to be able to say there were no casinos "in" Mississippi. On the other hand, nobody ever said things have to make sense, or if they did say it, I can't imagine who they were talking to.

I could smell the rich ocean fishiness, a smell of algae or I don't know what. It reminded me of vacations as a kid and other places, and the taste of salt. A ways off across a parking lot to the west was some sand with people on it, and I saw colored chairs and beach towels. I had an urge to go down to the sand and remove my shoes and socks, but if I did that Dove

would not know where I was. I didn't feel like going back into
the casino and tracking him down just so I could tell him I was
going to the beach.

I wished that instead of Dove it had been Mary in Biloxi
with me, and further I wished that she was in a red bathing
suit and that we were down there by the other people in the
sand and playing some kind of beach game with our son or
daughter. I could envision this scene and the different events
that would take place within it, like playing in the surf, building a castle, the handle coming off the cheap plastic bucket we
would have bought at a drugstore that morning, consoling the
child over the broken bucket handle, resting on towels, cleaning our feet before getting back into the car, picking out a
restaurant from the many along the beach, eating fried
shrimp, talking about how happy we were and what we would
do the next day, and so on. Maybe what I was doing was
remembering these things from my own childhood vacations
with family, except it didn't seem so, because it was Mary that
I envisioned at the table in the restaurant with her arms folded
at the edge of a checked tablecloth, then leaning across the
table to tend to the child.

There are several ways that small children look, and I
wondered what ours might have looked like had Mary had it,
instead of having her miscarriage. Would it have been one of
these chubby, fair-skinned kids, or would it have been one of
the darker-complected ones? Would he or she be skinny?
Bug-eyed or squinty-eyed? With a big broad forehead like
some of them have, or not so broad? I thought of something
which I had always known, and must have thought of many
times before, but it had never quite landed on me all the way
until now, and this was that even though Mary was pregnant
for only about two months, and in our heads it never got

much beyond an abstraction, or at least in my head it didn't—well, even so, inside her, the embryo or whatever one calls it did, while it was there, have its own set of genes and what have you. What I mean is, the whole thing could be viewed as if Mary and I had set down to a game of gin rummy and shuffled and dealt the cards but then before we had looked at our hands the cat knocked a plant over and we jumped up and the game never got played, and the cards went back into the deck and what our hands would have been, I mean *what our hands actually were,* was now a mystery and would never be known. In a similar way, I was thinking, though I could never know these certain things about the child we would have had, such as eye color, head shape, and native abilities, still I could be certain that each of these traits had been determined at one point. They were not known but they had existed and might have been known, if there had been a way to know them.

Well it was a highly interesting thought to me, though what difference it made I could not have explained. Clearly it made no difference, if it is agreed that things having no effect make no difference. But if the baby had at one time been real, then it was still real in one sense, was it not? Because there is a difference between something that never was and something that was. Philosophically the ins and outs were getting complex enough that I could tell I would soon be confused, if not already. I wondered when Dove was coming out, or if I would have to go in and find him in that throng. There were gulls around, chattering and moving about. Down below me in the parking lot a gull landed and stepped up to what appeared to be a french fry on the pavement, and was about to nab the fry when another gull landed alongside him and gave him a sharp peck in the eye.

The gull who had been pecked hopped backwards. The second gull, the pecker, stepped in and got the fry. I saw it all happen, and to my surprise a sensation of pressure rose in my chest and throat and I let out a sob like I had not done since I was nine years old.

Instantly I covered my mouth with my hand. I made sure the sob was over, and then my next move was to turn around quickly and look whether anyone was close by who might have heard me cry. There were people, but they were on the move and none of them were looking at me. There was a security guard at the door to the casino, but he was occupied clicking his counter as people came and went. I turned back to the parking lot and wiped my eyes, which were wet.

I was ashamed and startled, but at the same time I was outraged by that bastard second seagull. He was still down there, at least I thought it was him, digesting his stolen fry. The bird he had pecked was gone.

I looked around me for something to throw. Down the deck a few steps there was an ashtray, and someone had left a disposable lighter in it. I grabbed the lighter and leaned out over the deck rail and threw it sidearm, hard. I guess because of the passion of the moment and my intense concentration, I made a very accurate throw and clocked the seagull squarely on the back. He ducked in a panic, and then he gave a jump and flapped away.

23

THERE WAS A TAP ON MY SHOULDER, and I jumped around to see the security guard. He also jumped when I did. I sniffed and told him I would go retrieve the lighter and put it in the trash. "I was throwing it at a bird," I said.

He took a moment to settle, and then he asked me if my name was Wendell Brush.

"Yes."

"You're being paged," he said. "Didn't you hear?"

"No."

He talked on his radio. He then led me inside the casino and into a clot of people, at the middle of which was Dove, sitting on a bar stool glaring and being fanned with a metal clipboard by a female security guard. Dove didn't look at me. I asked the woman who was fanning him what was going on.

"This man had a fit," she said. "Are you Wendell?"

"Yes."

"Your friend decided to pick a fight with this gentleman here," she said. She pointed her finger at a fellow about my age who was rather short in stature but wiry, like a marathoner. He looked frightened. A few minutes earlier, I learned, he thought he had killed Dove. Dove had shoved him, and when he shoved back, Dove went down and began wheezing, curled up on the floor, and then went limp.

"I went to give him mouth-to-mouth," the wiry man said. Somebody laughed at him. The wiry man looked sad and confused. Dove was pouting and wouldn't speak.

I told the woman guard that all we needed to do was simply check in to one of the rooms at the casino hotel so that Dove could lie down and rest. She said that we were not especially invited to stay, but she would be glad to call Dove an ambulance. Dove sucked in a breath and said, "Hell no." At this the wiry man's mood changed again, and he threatened to pull Dove off the bar stool and knock him bloody. This brought more laughter from some considerate bystanders. Then a wheelchair appeared, and the guards put Dove in it and wheeled him to the front entrance. I brought the truck around, and we drove back west towards Gulfport and stopped at a hotel called the Grand Cabochon. Soon enough we were in a seventh-floor room with air-conditioning and a view across Highway 90 to the water.

My idea was for Dove to lie down, but what he did instead was set himself up at a round hotel-room table in a chair with his cigarettes and the remote. He switched on the television. I said, "You may as well go home, Dove, if smoke and watch television is all you're going to do."

"Don't have no home anymore," he said.

"Whose dumbass fault is that?"

"Yours."

"Mine?"

"Okay it's mine," he said. "How much is the beer by room service?" He was pointing to the menu by the telephone. I looked and couldn't tell, because the menu didn't give prices.

Dove held his hand out, grasping. "*Phone*," he said. I handed it to him.

He conferred with someone at his normal telephone volume, which was full volume. Then he said, "That's too high," and handed the phone back to me. "Wendell, will you please be my buddy and run get me two twelve-packs of Natural Light?"

"It's obvious that if I'm your buddy, that's exactly what I'm not going to do."

"Then will you be my worst enemy and run get me two twelve-packs please?"

The humorousness of continual drinking had begun to wear. I wasn't amused anymore by either of us. Dove was studying the remote, and I asked him what he was looking at. "Trying to figure out what all these buttons does," he said.

I took the remote from him and started clicking through the channels.

"I could have died a little while ago," Dove said. "Where were you at?"

"Getting some air. Who knew you'd be picking a fight with a wiry man?"

Dove asked me if I believed in the afterlife.

"I hope for your sake there's no hell," I said. I punched a button that made a small picture open up in the top right corner of the screen, allowing me to see two channels at once.

Dove said, "If a man has a soul, where is it at, and what is it attached to?"

"Too deep for me," I said.

I came to a car race and hit the button again quickly, hoping Dove would not have noticed, but of course he had. He said, "Whoa, cat. Back it up, there."

"This crap bores the crap out of me," I said.

"Too deep for you."

I put it back on the race, but I continued flipping channels in the little picture until I came to a man hooking cows up to a milking machine. That interested me, so I reversed things so that the cows were in the big picture and the car race in the little one.

Dove took the remote from me and reversed the pictures again. He continued switching channels in the small picture until he found a channel with nudity on. He said, "You know, if it wasn't for only one little detail that's missing from this moment, I could be the happiest man alive."

"What do you want?"

"I think you know what," he said. Straining, he cocked himself over onto one hip and worked his money roll out of his pocket. He gave me a twenty. "Be sure it's cold."

I went to the Grand Cabochon parking garage. While there, since no one was by, I got in the back of the truck, untaped and removed the sofa cushions and opened the convertible bed partway, and found the cash. It was wrapped in a blue plastic Wal-Mart bag. The bills were all hundreds, rubber-banded into eight flat bundles and reeking with that perfumey smell that paper money has. I made up my mind to take the cash to the front desk and have it placed in the hotel safe. But then I thought again, and wondered, What if Dove shoots himself? If the money is in the safe and Dove dies, then the money will have to be distributed by the court or something. Then I got aggravated that I was even having to worry about Dove and his money. I decided I didn't care what happened, and I wrapped the cash back in its bag and lifted the convertible bed frame to hide the money again.

But then I thought, What if somebody is lurking in this parking garage and has seen me handle the money? I looked at the wall, and there was a video camera pointing at me. Some hotel employee in a desk chair had been watching the whole time, and he was likely to be paying a visit to this truck at his first opportunity.

I was deeply annoyed at Dove and myself both. I taped the sofa cushions back in place and sat awhile, unhappy, in the back of the truck in the warm, dank parking garage. Then I went to the lobby and deposited the money in the safe, and then I went back to the truck and went out and bought a case of beer and two bags of Party Ice. When I got back to the room Dove was in bed asleep with the TV on. I filled the cooler and then went out to find something to do with myself.

24

I WENT TO THE BEACH and met a girl there, or young woman. She was twenty.

What happened was, I went down to the beach. It was late afternoon, past the hottest part of the day but still hot. I walked a long time, maybe a mile. The beach was without dunes and there was hardly any surf. There were many more birds than humans.

This was not the prettiest beach in the world. The water was brown, and storm drains emptied into it. At the mouths of the drains I found twigs, pine straw, and similar trash that had washed out from the streets. Still, it was a beach, with the overall saltiness and driftwood and vista and air, and to be plain, it was magnificent and made me miss Mary badly. I felt lonesome, pissed off, stupid, unhappy, and the rest.

I desired to remove my socks and shoes but had been putting it off because I didn't feel like carrying them. Then I thought, What's the likelihood of somebody making off with my socks and shoes? Would anyone want to even touch them, besides me? I left them in the sand and while I was at it, used my pocketknife to make cutoffs of my Dollar General pants. I slipped the lower halves of the pant legs off over my feet, and I walked another hour barefooted on the hard sand by the water.

I got to talking and gave a lecture to my imaginary child. The lecture was mostly on how it is best to be smart, and to appreciate what's given, and not screw everything up in life. I had plenty to say to the imaginary child on this subject. Then I stepped on a piece of bottle in the sand and slit the side of my foot open.

I sat down in the sand. "Look at this," I said.

"Ouch," somebody said.

I looked around me. Up from the water a bit, on a towel, was the young woman I have mentioned, in a blue bathing suit, sitting up hugging her knees. "Are you hurt?" she said.

"I cut my foot on some glass," I said. I pulled the piece of bottle out of the sand and held it up to show her.

She squinted at me. She had straight reddish hair, and her shoulders were becoming sunburned. She asked me could I walk.

"Sure I can," I said. I got up and walked back and forth, using only my heel on the cut side. "Good to go," I said.

She watched me demonstrate, and then she said "Okay" and went back to her sunning. I spied a garbage barrel a short ways off and limped over and deposited the piece of bottle in it.

When I looked back I saw her stand up and drop a dress on over her head. I limped back her way. She asked me how far I had to go, and I told her I was an hour from my shoes.

She pulled a ball cap on her head. She was a rather heavy girl of medium height, and pretty, with a look of youthful freshness about her. I was entertaining some improper thoughts about this young woman. "And then it's another mile past my shoes to the hotel," I said.

She said, "Are you carrying a knife or gun?"

I showed her my pocketknife. Fortunately I had already that morning taken Dove's bullets out of my pocket and thrown them in the trash at the IHOP.

"Give me that and I'll give it back to you," she said, and I handed it over. "Also, I'm very strong," she said. She laughed, but then she stopped laughing and said, "Seriously, I can hurt you."

"I understand," I said.

We went to her car, which was a maroon-colored Mazda that looked like it was on its ninth owner. She drove east on 90 then slowed down as much as was possible in traffic while I watched out the window for my shoes. I didn't spot the shoes, but I did remember what storm drain I had been by when I ditched them, and there was a parking bay near, so I had her stop there. I recovered the shoes, ignoring the pant-leg bottoms as though I had never seen them before. I carefully brushed my feet off and put the shoes on before getting back into the car.

I said, "By the way, my name is Don."

"My name is Nicole," she said.

We shook hands. She started laughing, and I asked her what she was laughing at. "The way you talk," she said.

"I'm from Tennessee," I said.

"That's not what I meant."

I told her I needed to go back to my hotel and do something about my foot, but after that I planned to find a restaurant and get supper, possibly someplace nice.

"That'll be nice, then," she said.

I asked her if she would like to come with me.

"I'm not sure that would be a good idea, actually."

"Okay," I said.

We nodded at each other. She checked the mirror for a gap in the traffic, but traffic was steady. "Is that it?" she said.

"That's good enough for me," I said.

"You give up pretty easy."

"Yes. I don't go in for multiplying turndowns, Nicole. Besides, I just remembered I don't have any clean clothes. I have one pair of brand-new socks that haven't been worn yet, and that's it. So I have no business being in a nice restaurant."

"But you're staying at the Grand Cabochon?"

"I'm not broke. I just don't have any clean clothes."

She frowned, watching traffic.

"You've got better things to do with your evening than to spend it with a codger like myself," I said.

A gray Crown Victoria eased by, leaving a gap, not a big one, and Nicole whipped the little Mazda out into the road. "I'm free tonight," she said. She pressed on over into the left lane, passing the slow-moving Crown Victoria, which was driven by an elderly gentleman. She gave him a stern look, but then he looked our way and she smiled at him. "It's very unusual for me to not have plans," she said. "Usually I've got my daughter, but she's with her father tonight, and his new girlfriend. But suppose we did go out, and we happened to go to the same restaurant as them? I know where they are, too! But your clothes."

"How old is your daughter?"

"Five." She reached behind her into a purse, in the floor of the backseat, and she pulled out her wallet and held it out to me, open to the plastic section with pictures. I took it from her and looked at her daughter, who was gorgeous, and grinning wildly. Adults don't grin that way, because they seldom find that kind of happiness to be warranted. I lost my mind and said out loud to myself, "Shit!"

I had forgotten Nicole was there, until she grabbed the wallet out of my hands. I looked up at her startled and she said, "You know what? You're an asshole." She hit her right-turn signal.

"Wait a minute," I said. "You misunderstand."

"I don't misunderstand!" she said. "I understand completely. You're like every other man, you're interested until you find out about the kid, and then you're not interested. You suck! But know this, you're kidding yourself anyway, because I'm not interested in you and wasn't ever. I only felt sorry for you, because you look like a hobo." She swerved right, into a parking bay, and stopped. "Get out of my car, you married loser."

"How did you know I'm married?"

She grabbed my ring finger and wrenched it up in my face.

"Look, I like children," I said. "I'm all for children. I don't want to talk about it, though."

She pulled the keys out of the ignition and held the key ring up in my face. "I'll pepper-spray you," she said.

I opened the door and tried to hop out but I had my seat belt on. "Wait, wait, let me get out," I said. I couldn't find the right thing to push, because I was not familiar with Mazda seat-belt fasteners. "Your daughter is very beautiful," I said. "Your daughter only makes you more attractive."

"What in the hell is that supposed to mean?"

I got my seat belt opened and got out of the car.

"Are you sick?" she said.

"No," I said. I stood well back from the car and leaned down to see her, but with my hand up to shield my eyes, should she choose to spray. "This is a misunderstanding."

"Maybe I should report you to the police."

"No, you don't understand," I said. "My wife isn't here. I'm normal. Your daughter is very pretty, and I don't mean that in an inappropriate way. I'm having trouble finding the correct way to say it, is all, because I'm not a good talker."

She put down the pepper spray and studied me. "You were doing okay on the beach," she said.

"What do you mean?"

"You were talking up a little storm out there."

"You're the one who started the conversation," I said.

"I mean before that. Before you stepped on the bottle. You were talking right out loud to yourself. I was looking for the TV cameras."

I stepped back from the car. I was embarrassed and now wished she would leave, but she put the keys back in the ignition and told me to get in. I did as she said and also put my seat belt back on.

I asked her, wasn't she afraid to have a jabbering maniac in her car?

"I'm not afraid of *you*," she said.

25

NICOLE QUICKLY RECOVERED from her angry outburst. "There's about fifteen separate kinds of creep that I have to be on watch for," she said. "The sex deviants, you know, they're the most worrisome with a five-year-old. But there's all kinds, like for example one guy, I went out with him twice and then he shows up at my apartment, we're watching television, and he suddenly sends out for pizza and then announces that his aquarium is out in the car, and he wants to move in with me. Right then, he wants to move in at that moment. I told him, 'What are you, a freeloader?' He says, 'Oh Nicole, I think I am falling *in love with you.*' I told him, 'We're going to eat this pizza and then you're leaving. You can take your fish to the Salvation Army.' I mean, imagine trying to freeload off a sales associate from Sears Brand Central. We don't make a great deal of money, okay? At least pick somebody from the middle class."

"I like Sears," I said. "My father buys only Craftsman tools."

She looked at me, and then at my shirt, and then back at the road.

"I had a thousand dollars' worth of mostly Craftsman tools stolen from my truck a while back," I said.

"That blows," she said. "So anyway, what are you doing here?"

"I'm just going with it," I said. "Whatever you want."

"I mean what are you doing in Biloxi."

"Oh. We came to drop off some furniture."

"You and who?"

"Me and my friend Dove. That's who I'm staying with."

"So why are you staying at the Grand Cabochon? That's kind of a fancy hotel for some furniture movers."

"Dove has money. We're not really deliverymen by profession."

"What are you, drug dealers?"

"Not to my knowledge."

"Is this Dove guy married? That's a funny name, Dove. Are you homosexual?"

"I'm not, and neither is he. And no, he's not married."

"Does he have a fascination with Craftsman tools?"

"I think he would like you, Nicole. But he's a sixty-nine-year-old man in the body of an eighty-year-old."

She considered that. "Looks and age don't count for much with me, Don," she said. She laughed lightly. She asked me what I did for a living.

"I'm an electrician, when I'm working."

"An electrician."

"Do you think I'm lying?"

"You don't seem like an electrician. You seem like some kind of a Chilean mystic."

"I don't know what that means," I said. "Are you making fun of me?"

"No, but I don't think you look like an electrician. Those

pants. You look more like somebody who would maybe work at a zoo. I could see you nursing baby animals."

"You want to take me to your house and I'll put in a fixture for you?"

"I haven't known you long enough," she said. "Anyway, we're here."

She was pulling into the lot of the Grand Cabochon. She parked, and we got out. I asked her across the purple roof of her car where she was going. "Up to meet your friend," she said.

"He was in bed when I left," I said. "He's sick. They almost called the paramedics for him at the casino today."

"What's wrong with him?"

"He collapsed. He's just beat up, from hard living over the years."

We stood in the parking lot as seagulls yipped and swooped above our heads. It was very hot on the asphalt by the hot car. I looked up at the windows of the hotel, with the glare on them from the sun, which was low. Nicole pulled her hair back off her neck and put an elastic thing around it. She looked at me. Her face was damp from sweating.

"If he's that bad off what are you doing walking around all over the beach all afternoon?" she said.

We went inside the hotel and up to the room. We found Dove standing in the floor fully dressed, freshly shaved, and holding the remote control.

"Dove, this is Nicole," I said. "Nicole, this is Dove."

He stubbed out a cigarette and coughed lowly. "Hello Nicole," he said.

"Hello Dove." She stood back near the door and looked around at the room.

I told Dove he was looking better. He had on a clean striped shirt and he had even ironed it, as I could tell because the hotel iron was out on the dresser top, and I could also smell ironing.

"I do what I can with what little I've got," he said. "I'm pleased to meet you, Nicole."

I said, "If you'll excuse me, I'm going to see about my foot."

"What's wrong with your foot?" Dove said.

"I cut it on the beach, and that's how I met Nicole."

"All he had to do was say hello," Nicole said.

"Wendell's got his own way of doing everything," Dove said.

"Who's Wendell?" Nicole said.

"The one you come in with."

I asked Dove where my new socks were that I had bought.

Dove asked Nicole if she would like a beer.

"Why yes, thank you," she said. She stepped further into the room.

"Are you old enough?"

I asked Dove again about my socks. He said, "Did you look in the drawer?" Of course he knew I had not looked in the drawer, because we were all standing in one room not more than eighteen feet on each side. Everybody could see plainly what everybody else was doing. I went to the dresser and opened a drawer, and there were all of Dove's clothes folded in flat squares and arranged. I looked in the next drawer and there was my pair of white tube socks, the adhesive-paper label still wrapped around them.

"Wendell ain't never seen clothes kept in a drawer before," Dove said.

I went into the bathroom, shut the door, and looked in the mirror. I looked ill and sunstruck. I sat down and uncovered my foot, which was not nice to see. It made me think of cleaning fish. I turned the shower on, and another pair of socks went into the trash.

As long as I was showering my foot, I might as well get all the way in, I decided. There was a knock on the door and I said "Yes?" and Dove stuck his head in. He said, "What are you doing taking a shower?"

"You answered your own question," I said.

Dove took his head away and said to Nicole, "He's in the shower!" He opened the door all the way.

She came to the door and stood behind him. "Don, why are you in the shower?" she said.

"I'm dirty," I said. I was standing away from the shower curtain, which was green and somewhat transparent, and I stuck my head out to see them.

"Get out of the shower, Wendell," Dove said. "You have company."

"My foot is cut," I said. "Shut the door."

"Let me see that," Dove said.

"This is a little weird," Nicole said.

Dove came in and put his head past the shower curtain and looked at my foot. He said, "Son, you need to put some iodine on that before you lose the foot."

"I'm not going to lose the foot," I said.

"I could pour some beer on it."

I checked what Nicole was doing and saw her looking at herself in the mirror.

"Please, Dove," I said.

"Here, take this," he said. He handed me his beer.

"I'm not putting beer on my foot!" I said. "A little privacy!"

"No, I want you to drink it," Dove said. "It's yours, I ain't sipped it. What's wrong with you, Wendell?"

"Nothing's wrong with me except my foot is cut and I could use some privacy for a minute."

He sniffed and then he turned and tapped Nicole on the shoulder. They exited the bathroom and shut the door.

I cleaned my foot and then got out, dried off, and put on my clean socks and my other dirty clothes and slipped out the bathroom and into the hallway. I rode the elevator down to the lobby and found a pay phone and dialed my number in Tennessee, then hung up after one ring. I went to a sofa and sat down and in a minute, a security guard came over and asked me if he could help me.

"I'm fine," I said.

He asked me if I was a guest.

"What do you mean? Yes I'm a guest. I'm staying here."

He asked my room number, and I couldn't remember it. I had left without my key card. I told him so, and I told him I was staying with Dove Ellender, and he asked me who I was talking to. "I'm talking to you," I said. "The security guard."

"I mean before I stepped over. You were talking to someone."

"No I wasn't."

He said, "If you're some kind of undercover agent, we appreciate being apprised of that sort of operation prior to it taking place. We want to know what's going on in our hotel."

He was a small man. He might have been a boy almost. He had a slight mustache and pale hair, and he was leaning in towards me whispering.

"I'm not a secret agent," I said.

He nodded. "I thought you might be, because of the way you appeared to be talking to yourself."

"I've recently stopped drinking," I said.

"I hear you. But if you would, please stop talking to yourself, or go out of the lobby. Or both."

"I will. Thank you."

"No, thank *you*," he said.

I rode the elevator up, got off on the wrong floor, limped up a flight of stairs, and found the room, recognizing it by a cigarette burn on the carpet near the door. I knocked and Nicole let me in with a questioning look. Dove was at the table, and Nicole sat down in a chair and put her feet up on the bed as though returning them to the spot where they had been before I knocked.

"I ain't seen that one since he was twelve," Dove was saying.

He looked at me, drawing on his cigarette, and then frowned and set the cigarette in the ashtray. He let out a long stream of smoky breath.

Nicole was also smoking. "How many have you got?" she said.

"Three. One that speaks to me. Or she did, before yesterday."

"What's she mad about?"

"I offered her some money if she would leave her husband."

"You what?" I said.

Nicole said, "That made her mad, did it?"

"Honey, she was hot. She sounded like her mother, too. It was a flashback to the past." Then he looked at me and said, "Why don't you set down, Igor?"

I sat down on the far bed.

"I guess I'm a dumbass," he said. He was talking to Nicole, not me. "I knowed it since a long time ago, and I just need to accept it. The thing is, because you're a dumbass don't mean you don't have ideas. They're dumb ideas, but you don't know that when you have them."

"I've known some dumbasses," Nicole said. She snorted.

"There's a lot of us about," Dove said. "I never minded being a dumbass, but being an old dumbass kind of gets to me. It's being a can't-walk dumbass, you see. Well, I said I wasn't going to bitch no more, though." He raised his bottle and shook it—it was empty. He set it down and held out his hand to me in a bottle-holding shape. I got a bottle out of the ice chest and uncapped it and put it in his hand.

I said, "So that's what the brouhaha was over."

Dove squinted at me. "Where'd you get that word 'brouhaha'?"

"I learned it in the fourth grade."

"You must have been out sick that day, Dove," Nicole said.

"I was out, but I wasn't sick."

They laughed.

"So then when she wouldn't leave Jimbo, you told her she couldn't have any of your money. You're stupid, Dove."

"I just said it was stupid, Wendell. Hey Wendell, me and Nicole's working out a deal."

"Shut up!" Nicole said, laughing.

"I told her I'd give her two hundred dollars to pull her top down, and she said all right, and now I'm trying to talk her down to a hundred."

"I'm not doing it for a hundred," she said.

"I better leave for a minute," I said.

"Where are you going?" Dove said.

I got up off the bed. In the glass doors to the balcony I could see the three of us reflected. That was because it was turning dusky outside. In particular I noticed the reflection of Nicole's long, straight, reddish-gold hair. It was a way of staring at her hair without her knowing it. "Maybe I'll get us some food," I said.

"You're going to miss it, Wendell. I'm about to close the deal."

Nicole smiled. I looked at her and she looked straight back at me for a second, then looked away. I didn't know what she was thinking, but the idea that she might be at some point willing to have sex with me did cross my mind. Or to be accurate, it crossed halfway, then stopped and stayed.

26

I WENT TO THE COOLER and dug myself out a beer.

"I am so damn relieved," Dove said. "You don't make a good teetotaler, Wendell. You were turning bug-eyed."

I opened my beer and took a long pull. The familiarity of it was a great comfort. Also, a beer from the ice chest is always better than one from the fridge.

Dove and Nicole got back to the subject of Dove's offspring. He had a son named Terry who was an osteopathic physician in Colorado and another named Jeff whose whereabouts he didn't know. Terry was the oldest. His mother and Dove were both teenagers when he was born, and he'd been mostly raised by his maternal grandparents in Kingsport, who were very fine people, Dove said, and smart not to have let him near their grandson.

"Not at all?" Nicole said.

"I was not around in a fatherly role. Hell, he's fifty-two now. He could be your father."

"I wouldn't mind having a doctor for a father."

"Good luck getting any money out of him," Dove said. "Of

course, he's earned every penny of it. He works his hind end off."

Nicole asked Dove how many times he'd been married.

"Four times."

"I thought it was three," I said.

"Do you think I ought to know how many times I was married?"

"You ought to, but I question whether you do."

"Come here so I can hit you," Dove said.

"Don't hit Don," Nicole said.

"Why not?"

"He's gentle."

"I'm not gentle," I said.

"Yes you are. Be nice to him, Dove."

"All right," Dove said. "I'll be nice to him, since he's a gentle boy."

"I like gentle boys," Nicole said.

"Let's cut this out," I said. I finished my beer and got another. I offered one to Nicole.

"If I drink any more without eating I'll be drunk," she said.

"I'm already light-headed," Dove said.

Nicole stood up and smoothed her dress with her hands. I thought of the bathing suit that she was wearing beneath it, and I was attracted to her. She had taken her shoes off and now she tripped over one of them and fell beside me on the bed. We bumped heads.

"Ouch!" she said.

It hurt. Her forehead had bounced off of my left temple.

"Sorry about that," she said. She got up and went off to the bathroom and shut the door.

"That was on purpose," Dove said.

"I don't think so," I said. I held my temple. "She smells good."

"Awfully good," Dove said.

I told him I was going to run out to the liquor store real quick.

"Are you skittish?"

"Maybe."

"What you ought to do is get your own room," he said.

"By myself?"

"I mean with Nicole," he said.

It was a logical suggestion, but it surprised me. I asked him, "Why would I want to do that?"

He looked me up and down and shook his head. He said, "I don't know why you won't admit certain things."

I considered his long gray head and neatly coiffed hair. In a way he resembled a horse, and I told him that.

"I've heard it before," he said.

Outside the hotel, the evening was bright with the street-lights, lot lights, and colored signs and surfaces of Biloxi. The liquor store, which I'd had the foresight to notice earlier, even though I had given up drinking at the time I noticed it, was two lots down from the hotel. I cut through parking lots to get there, and I purchased a big jug of Henry McKenna on the Visa check card. While standing outside the liquor store crinkling the top of the paper sack around the neck of the bottle I had another idea, and I hiked two more lots down to a Shell station, where I bought some protection, I mean rubbers.

Coming back I paused in an empty parking space between two white Grand Cabochon vans and twisted the plastic cap off the jug and had a sip. I wondered what Mary had been eating since I left. It was Thursday, so therefore I had been gone for five suppers, or six if she had eaten already this evening. Her favorite meal was tortellini, not boxed but the kind that comes refrigerated in a plastic container. I wondered if she had been eating nothing but tortellini all week. She sometimes would drink a glass of red wine with it, but rarely more than one. We always watched television while we ate.

I sat down on the curb. I noticed a nickel on the pavement between my shoes but did not pick it up. I wasn't a rich person, but at some point in life I had stopped picking up change off the pavement. I drank another warm swallow of bourbon. I let perhaps thirty minutes tick by in this way, with me thinking my interesting thoughts and smelling the night. On 90 the traffic was voluble. The people who like their vehicles to be noisy were out burning up clutches and tire rubber.

I arose to my feet good and wobbly and went back into the glowing hotel lobby and into the men's room, where I washed my hands and swished out my mouth with water. Then I mounted the elevator and rode up and found the room, and I let myself in with the key card, which I had remembered this time.

Nobody was in the room. The ashtray had been emptied into the wastebasket and the TV was off. The glass door to the balcony, which had been open a couple of inches to let the smoke out, was open all the way. I went to step out there and have a look at the night from above, but when I got close the height made me nervous and I didn't step past the doorsill. I shut the door and locked it.

I heard coughing from the bathroom.

"Dove?" I said.

"In a minute," he said back.

When he came out I said, "Where's Nicole?"

"She says good night."

I got a glass from the bathroom, pulled the wrapper off, and poured myself a drink. I offered Dove one and he wouldn't answer. I took the box of rubbers from the paper bag and tossed it onto the dresser top, where it slid, then stopped against the mirror.

"You're completely lost," Dove said.

27

I DRANK ALL I COULD, and in the morning I paid for it. This was truly a deluxe hangover, tricked out with all of the options and a couple of custom features. It started at four A.M. when I woke suddenly with a feeling of serious dread. My face was clammy and a renegade nose hair obstructed my breathing. I smacked at my nose, but I couldn't get the nose hair to straighten.

Then I became aware of a nausea. I went into the bathroom hoping to vomit, but it was not to be yet. I got back in bed and watched CNN with the sound off. I was comforted a little and became sleepy, and when it started getting daylight from the glass doors I switched off the television. I tried lying very still, and then I put a pillow under my knees.

My head began to throb, and I felt as though there were sharp shreds of foil behind my eyes and nose. I tossed in the bed. Dove sat up and asked me what in the hell was going on, and I told him I couldn't sleep, and he told me to stop thrashing. A few minutes later he got in the shower and the steam brought out the smell of last night's cigarettes, and I wanted to die.

When he got out, Dove said he was going down for break-fast. He asked me if I was coming and I said, "No."

"I feel so relaxed after making love to Nicole last night," he said.

"You did not."

"Oh yes I did, while you were gone. You want me to describe her body?"

"Shut up and go away," I said.

He left and I got sick. Then I slept some more. Afternoon came and I got dressed, walked down the hall, and bought a pack of Nabs from a machine. I got back in bed and ate a Nab.

Dove came in saying "Wendell, we have trouble."

"What is it?"

"Are you awake? I don't want to go through this twice."

"I'm awake," I said.

"Open your eyes."

I did it.

"I ran into a bookie and put some money on Jeff Gordon."

"I thought you hated Jeff Gordon," I said.

"So what?"

"Did Gordon lose?"

"Today's Friday," Dove said.

"So?"

"So the race has not took place yet, Wendell. The problem is, I went to my truck, and the money ain't there."

"I got it out yesterday," I said. "It's in the safe at the front desk."

"You did that?"

"Yes. I meant to tell you yesterday but you were asleep, and then I forgot. You thought it was stolen?"

"I just seen it was gone," he said.

"Did you think I had stolen it?"

"No."

He was calmer than I would have been, had I been missing thirty-eight thousand dollars. "How much did you bet, anyway?"

"Fifteen."

I got up out of the bed again and brushed my teeth. I was alarmed to see that my spit was orange, until I remembered the Nab. I said to Dove, "You mean fifteen thousand?"

"Yep."

"That's not too smart, is it?"

"I think it's real damn smart."

"Gordon's been winning?"

"He don't have to win. He has to qualify in the top three."

I sat down in a chair in my underwear. I pushed down on the top of my head. Dove stood like a cowbird by the dresser in his jeans and short-sleeved striped shirt and neatly combed hair, watching me.

"What odds does that give you?" I said.

"Fair odds."

"It doesn't sound good, though."

"Probably it ain't, Wendell. What difference does it make to you?"

"None, I guess. If you want to be stupid, be stupid."

He sniffed. He opened a drawer and took out a small white paper bag, from which he produced a cardboard box. He picked at the cellophane on the box and peeled it away. It clung to his fingers and he flicked it onto the carpet. He slid a small canister out of the box and inserted it into his plastic inhaler, and he gave himself a suck of it in the mouth.

He shut his eyes. He said, "You're starting to bug me and piss me off, Wendell."

"I don't care."

"I'm tired of looking after you. I want my money."

"They'll only give it to me," I said. "I'm the one that signed it in."

"I'm aware of that."

"What do you mean, you're tired of looking after me? I've been looking after you."

"The day's half gone and you're not dressed, Wendell. You look like hell. When you're dressed, you still look like hell with your cut-up pants and dirty shirts. You don't shave. Why'd you bring that girl up last night and then run off?"

"Leave me alone about that," I said. "She did all right without me, according to you."

"You hurt her feelings, asshole. That was another human being. Go get my money now before this gets ugly."

I put my dirty clothes on. Dove called someone on the phone and said, "We're coming. We'll meet you in the lobby by the elephant-ear plant." He hung up and I asked him what made him believe he could trust this bookie with fifteen thousand dollars.

"I trust nobody," he said.

We rode the elevator down and when the doors opened a seven-foot pole of a man was waiting. He was perhaps sixty, with a stooping posture and a shaved head. He looked at me.

"I said by the big green plant," Dove said. He walked on past the man toward the front desk, and I followed.

At the desk I showed my receipt and the cashier brought out Dove's money in a tray. Dove counted out 150 hundreds and put these into an envelope provided by the cashier. He put the remaining hundreds into a second envelope which he tried to insert in his front jeans pocket, but he couldn't work it in. He handed it to me and said, "Put this somewhere."

"Leave that in the safe," I said.

"Please do as I ask," he said.

I shoved it in my pocket. We went to the big green plant at the other end of the lobby, where the tall man was obediently waiting. He had on gray pants and a white short-sleeved shirt, and he wore military dress shoes. He looked like a bald guy who had taught science at my high school, except on a 130 percent scale. Dove said, "Let's ride the elevator," and the man followed us in. Dove gave him the envelope and he took out the money and counted it very slowly, twice.

"Is it all there?" Dove said.

"Just barely," the man said.

I said, "So you're a real-life bookmaker. What's that like?"

"I'm not a bookmaker. That's illegal," he said.

Dove said, "Wendell, shut the hell up."

I said, "How do you feel about taking a man's money that he's worked hard for? Do you know you're holding half a life's savings right there?"

The man looked at the money and then at Dove.

Dove said, "You're about to cross a line, Wendell."

I watched Dove's head turn purple. The vessels in his neck stood up.

"I don't care," I said. "I'm in an elevator in Mississippi and I don't mind telling both of you that this is wrong behavior and needs to stop." I reached up and pushed down on the top of my head. I put out my other hand and said, "Give me the money back and we'll forget this nonsense."

The tall man moved the envelope behind his back.

"You keep that money!" Dove said. "The deal's on!"

I asked Dove not to yell.

The tall man said to Dove, "Who is this person?"

"I'm his friend, and you're his parasite," I said.

"I've never been called a parasite," the man said.

The bell dinged and the elevator stopped. A woman and a girl of about eight got on. They were made up and had their hair done so they looked like twins in two sizes. They smiled identically as we descended. Dove was deep in a mute baby bird, quivering. The floor numbers lit up and at the third floor the tall man asked Dove, "Are we going ahead with this?"

Dove blinked and swallowed and then he said, "Yes. You do exactly as we said." His voice sounded far away, like a cricket in a shoe.

At "L," the door opened and the tall man got off. The woman went next, and then her small twin, who as she left turned to look at me over her shoulder. She stuck out her lips in a quick, noiseless goodbye kiss.

Something hit me in the ear then. My head snapped to the right and I fell onto the elevator wall. It was Dove, or more precisely Dove's fist. He stood over me now with a look of congestion on his face. He sputtered.

I held up my arm and Dove swung at it. He lost his balance and went down like some badly stacked firewood. The elevator door was closing and it squeezed him around the shoulders then slid back open. Dove rolled onto his side and curled up.

A man with a hotel name badge appeared. Dove's mouth was open, his lips pulled back. He wouldn't speak. I was somewhat disoriented until the man who was kneeling by Dove's head told me to hold down the DOOR OPEN button. I did as he said. The man asked Dove to sit up.

Dove turned his head a little. He said, "Oh shit. Am I alive?"

"Right now you are," the man said. He helped Dove up slowly and got him to a plush chair.

The hotel man asked me what had happened.

I was holding my head and slow to answer. Dove said, "The bastard pushed me down!"

"Me?" I said.

The hotel man glared at me and got on his walkie-talkie.

"I did not knock him down," I said. "He hit me in the ear."

"You cruel bastard," Dove said. "Go away from me. I don't ever want to see you again."

"He's not well," I said. People were gathering.

"I can see he's not well," the hotel man said.

At that, Dove began croaking in an exaggerated way. He patted all of his pockets as though he was searching for his inhaler. This was a sham, I knew, because he always kept the inhaler in his shirt pocket with his cigarettes. People groaned in sympathy with him.

If I wasn't wanted, I'd leave. I tugged the fat envelope with Dove's cash in it out of my pocket, and I plunked it down on his lap. He started back with pretend fear.

"What is that?" the hotel man said.

People gasped as though I'd produced a bomb. "It's his envelope," I said. "I was holding it for him."

Dove took a long, dramatic suck from his inhaler. He held up his hand to indicate that he had something to say as soon as he was able. All were quiet. Dove made several pained and sour expressions, and then he picked up the envelope and said, "I have never seen this envelope, nor this person."

The hotel man grabbed the envelope. His eyes got narrow as he felt of it, but then he made his mind up and shoved it at me. "Take this and start walking," he said.

"It isn't mine."

"Take it or I'll call the police," he said.

I took it. Then I asked him where he wanted me to walk to.

He pointed backwards. "Out the door," he said.

Uniformed guards had come. One of them whispered something to the man with the name badge, and he grabbed my arm. He asked Dove, "Sir, would you like to pursue charges?"

"Old people aren't safe!" I heard a lady say.

Dove pretended to think, and then he moved his big head slowly. "No. Just so I don't ever see him again, please."

28

OUTSIDE THE HOTEL the day was bright and made my skull creak. I felt my way through the sunlight and when I got to the edge of the parking lot, I turned and said goodbye out loud to Dove and the Grand Cabochon Hotel.

I moved west on the sidewalk. My head throbbed, and my ear burned where Dove had boxed it. I put my hands over my eyes and that helped some until a large boy in flip-flops who was following his parents while reading a paperback bumped into me, causing me to spin halfway and feel dizzy. I stopped and swayed for a while.

Nearby was the liquor store I had patronized the previous night. People talk about hair of the dog. I went in and explained that I had a terrible hangover and asked the cashier what was recommended.

She reached into a cabinet and with a loud clack slapped down on the counter a plastic bottle of aspirin.

"How much?" I said.

"Start with two."

I swallowed two dry. The cashier squinted at me as the aspirins went down.

Back out in the sun I reached by habit into my pocket for my knife, which I like to hold. Of course it wasn't there. I had just about rather lose my billfold than my knife. There are many stories of lives saved by the stroke of a sharp pocketknife blade. Some are grisly, like the one about the man who got his arm hung up in a thresher or some kind of farm implement and had to cut the last band of tissue so he could go to the house and call 911. I had repeated this story several times to Mary when I caught her not carrying the small Gerber locking-blade knife that I gave her, and she always replied that a cell phone would have helped the man more than his knife did, so why didn't I get her a cell phone? I had meant to and meant to and never had done it. Now I regretted that. A man with a knife and a woman with a cell phone make a formidable combination.

I studied my frame of mind and found that I was not as torn up as I would have expected, given the circumstances. I would have been glad to place my head in a carton and stow it far from my body, but otherwise I was tolerating this new twist fairly well. I supposed I could get along somehow without Dove's conversation. Having twenty-three thousand dollars of his money in my pocket was an interesting novelty.

Why should things carry on the same way from one moment to the next? It seems there is something about life that causes a person to expect this when he ought not to. A dog is the same way, cherishing his routine. My limited experience with chickens told me that they were no different.

I walked a long while and decided I would use Dove's money to buy a truck. I had grown too accustomed, it struck me, to not expecting the best for myself. Hope frightens people because to hope, you have to imagine a better world. We should always know that hazards are real, and we should cultivate hope and exploit each opportunity for improvement. I knew many friends who drove big new trucks and deserved them no more than I did.

I had noticed numerous dealerships on the trip down, entering Gulfport on 49. At most it would be a twenty-mile walk, not a problem since I had the rest of my life uncommitted. I had gone a hundred yards when I decided to step into a place called Ape Man's Souvenirville, where I inspected a desk lamp made of seashells and noted that it lacked the UL listing. There's no law saying that an appliance must be tested by Underwriters Laboratories before it is sold. If I wanted to make my own line of toasters out of roof metal and sell them at the flea market, there'd be no one to stop me. On my way out I purchased a small replacement pocketknife that said BILOXI DEER RANCH on the side in enamel. It was the type of knife that comes in a manicure kit and it was sharp enough to crease a sheet of notebook paper. I found a concrete bench outside and took a seat on the edge of it and began grinding the blade against a smooth spot on the concrete, using care to maintain the critical 15-degree angle. The blade was chrome-plated, but the chrome wore off with a few strokes.

I'm happy sharpening. With my other eye I counted Chevys. Nine late-model full-size Chevy pickups passed in two minutes. When I say "Chevy" I am including GMCs. Then I switched and counted nine Fords, which took somewhat longer. The GMs were the truck of choice on Highway 90 in Biloxi. I didn't do a Dodge count because I had already ruled them out.

I wondered if I would be happy with one of the new full-size Toyotas. The word was that they had power but lacked the leg- and headroom of the American full-size trucks. I spotted a Toyota that was the same year-model as mine, an '84, and I thought as I often had that it was a smart-looking vehicle.

They were good on gas and easy to drive in town, and really the size was sufficient for my needs. I missed my truck. The particular one that I was watching go by had a curly-haired woman in eyeglasses driving it. Her truck was an unusually bright blue, a shade better suited to a tropical fish than to a pickup, in my opinion.

Then she was gone. Her face had seemed extremely familiar. I closed my knife—it didn't close well—and I started walking back towards the Grand Cabochon. I ran. Then I had to walk again, because of my foot. At the hotel I climbed a planter to scan the parking lot. I didn't see the Toyota so I climbed down and started for the main entrance, and then I saw it, parked near the front. I ran to it and looked in the window.

On the seat was a black overnight bag, the same one I had rifled through on Saturday. I tried the door, and it was locked, but I had the key to it in my pocket.

29

I LET MYSELF IN on the passenger side. On the seat by the bag there was a road map of the Southeast, a new one misfolded and mangled in Mary's characteristic way, which I knew well and had always believed that I hated, though it seemed to me now that I loved it. She had traced out the route from Johnson City to Biloxi with a green highlighter pen.

I rolled down both windows and sat with my arm on her overnight bag, watching towards the hotel entrance a hundred yards off, where I assumed she had gone. Twenty minutes went by. Then I saw her coming. I knew her at first by her stride. The hair was bouncy in all directions. I got out and stood beside the truck, and when she saw me she stopped for a second, then came on.

She stopped again twelve feet away. "Why are you standing out here?" she said.

"Waiting for you."

"I've been in there with Dove trying to figure out where to find you."

She had on a black sleeveless top that was new to me. The

khaki shorts with cuffs in them I recognized. Her hair would take some getting used to. The stubble from the SeamerMate accident was well concealed.

"Where did those pants come from?" she said.

"I bought them."

She came a few steps closer. My breath was made quick and my pulse jumped as though I had eaten several sugar cubes. Her cheeks and neck were blotched with redness.

I asked her how she had found us.

"Dove called me last night. Didn't you know I was coming?"

"No. I just spotted the truck, just now."

"It stands out," she said.

"Do you like it?"

"It's ugly, Don."

Mary was pretty. That I had forgotten just how pretty made me wonder what I'd done to myself in the week since I'd last seen her. She looked tired. She had driven six hundred miles. Her tired eyes were immensely beautiful with their intelligence and expressiveness and their unmistakable Maryness. She was like nobody else, ever. I was dotty.

"Dove's not happy," Mary said.

"I know it. Mary, I love you," I said.

She seemed to be studying my face. "Are you okay?"

"I'm wonderful."

"Dove says you're acting strangely."

"Well?"

"I mean disturbed. He says you're spaced out and muttering. And you're sunburned. Where's your hat?"

"Something happened to it," I said. It had fallen under the seat in Dove's truck, and then I didn't want to wear it anymore.

"Let's go somewhere," she said. "Somewhere air-conditioned."

She drove. I looked at and admired the slightly raised blood vessels on the back of her hand as she handled the gear shift.

"I love my truck," I said. "I'm never going to trade."

"The oil light came on in the car," she said.

"That's not good. Did you pull over right away?"

"Yes."

"Did you have it towed?"

"It's in the shop."

"The oil light," I repeated.

"Tell me what's going on," she said.

"It could be the oil pump."

I reflected. I asked her exactly what time Dove had called and what all he had said. The gist of it was that he had told her I was drinking too much and was a threat to myself and needed rescuing immediately. As for time, it appeared that he had called either while Nicole was in the room or shortly after she had left. Mary said nothing about a female being involved. I was terrified to think what I might have done with Nicole, had things gone differently.

"I guess Dove's had enough of me," I said.

"If that was all, he could have put you on a bus," Mary said.

"Did you call in sick to work today?" It was Friday.

"I've been out sick all week, Don."

"Were you sick?"

"I'll be all right."

I asked her if we were getting back together.

She shook her head and didn't say anything.

I reached and turned on the tape player, and she turned it off. "Please," she said. "I've had twelve hours of Johnny Rivers." There was a Johnny Rivers tape stuck in the player.

She swung us off 90 and we went into a restaurant. We got a booth in a corner under a wooden rowboat that hung from the ceiling. It was late afternoon, and the other tables were empty. We ordered iced tea and Mary asked me why I hadn't come into the hotel when I found my truck in the parking lot.

"Oh! Look here," I said. I had remembered the envelope. I pulled it out of my pocket and set it on the table. "Look inside there."

As Mary was looking, the waiter came back with our iced tea. She smiled blandly at him. I ordered a cheeseburger, and Mary got a salad.

When the waiter left, Mary's smile disappeared and she pushed the envelope back at me. "Put this away," she said.

"It doesn't fit very well in my pocket," I said. "There's two hundred and thirty hundreds there."

She frowned and stuck it into her purse. "Where did this come from?"

"It's Dove's."

"Why do you have it?"

"I was holding it for him, and then he wouldn't take it back."

"You mean he gave it to you?"

"He denied it was his."

"You've got to take it back to him."

"I was trying to give it back when he said he never wanted to see me again. He pretended not to know me, and then he pretended he couldn't breathe. They told me to leave the hotel."

"Who did?"

"Some man with a name tag." I filled her in on the whole business, from the Jeff Gordon bet up through my ejection from the lobby.

"I don't understand," Mary said. "I just talked to Dove, and he didn't say anything about this money. Where did he get it?"

"He sold his house."

She looked worried. "I'm going to wash my hands," she said.

I watched her scoot out of the seat and cross the room, cutting between tables with her purse clutched to her side. She went to the waiter, who was hunched at a table doing math, and he pointed her the right way. I watched her cross again, never so thankful in my life to see another person. Even if we did have to split up, I thought, I could live with it, because knowing that Mary was in the world was enough to make anyone grateful.

30

WHEN SHE CAME BACK to the table she said, "I have some bad news to tell you, Don."

"What?"

"A truck ran into our house," she said.

"A truck?"

"Yes."

"What happened?"

"It drove through the fence and into the corner of the house."

"Which corner?"

"The back corner by the road. It was coming down the hill from the Crumleys' house and it went off the road to avoid George."

"George Massey?"

"George was backing his truck into our driveway, and the other truck ran off the road to miss him."

"And it ran into our house?"

"There's a drop-off on the other side."

"Why was George backing into our driveway?" I said.

"He's been coming by the house every day."

"Why?"

"To check on me or something. You left."

"He doesn't need to check on you. What's he meddling for? He's eighty years old."

"He's just been coming by, Don."

"So you were there when it happened?"

"Yes."

"How bad is it?"

"He hit the house. There's damage. Take it easy, now."

"I am," I said. I took a few breaths. "Was the driver hurt?"

"Not in the least."

"Was he going fast? Was it that son, Rastus or whatever? The bastard!"

"It wasn't a Crumley. It was a man they had up there cutting trees."

"What kind of trees?"

"Big trees. Oaks."

"What kind of truck was it?"

"I don't know. One of those trucks they haul trees with."

"A log truck ran into our house?"

"Yes."

"Oh shit!" I got up out of the booth and stood. "Is there anything left of the house?"

"I've been staying in it."

"So it's not too bad, then?"

"The lights don't work in the living room, and one of the front doors won't open."

"Oh shit!"

"Look, it's the least of our troubles right now," she said.

"No, it's not the least of our troubles! This is going to be one of our main troubles."

"Sit down," she said.

I did. "I guess that whole corner is caved in," I said.

"Not completely. Look, I want to talk about something else."

"What?"

"We've got to have a meeting with Tommy Maudlin."

"Who is Tommy Maudlin?"

"The lawyer. I told you."

"You told me you were going to a lawyer, but you never told me his name was Tommy Maudlin."

Our food came. We were quiet while the waiter set the plates down and asked us whether we needed anything else right then.

"No thank you," Mary said.

When he was gone I said, "You don't need a lawyer, Mary. You can have everything. I don't care."

"I don't want everything."

"Have what you want, then."

"That's not how it works," she said. "We're not dividing assets, we're dividing liabilities."

"What do you mean by that?"

"The student loans are mine, but we owe thirty-four hundred on the car, and we owe twenty-four thousand on the house. The house needs some work, Don. We owe eighteen hundred on the credit card. We'll have to split these up."

"Oh. Well we have assets too," I said.

"Like your four lawn mowers."

"I use three of them every week," I said.

"I know it. George Massey wants to buy a lawn mower from you."

"I can't do that."

"Come on, Don. They're lawn mowers."

"That's how that's going to be," I said. "Let him go to Sears and buy a mower."

She was holding her fork, and she looked into her salad. She set the fork down and drank some iced tea.

I asked her what she was thinking.

"How difficult this is," she said.

"You're handling it very calmly."

"What do you want me to do? Cry?"

"If you think it's appropriate."

"I've been crying all week," she said. "If you wanted to see crying you should have stayed home."

"I don't want to see crying."

"Why'd you leave?"

"I left because you were leaving."

"I wasn't leaving the state," she said. "I wasn't disappearing. I wanted out of the house is all."

"I know you did. I didn't want you to leave the house."

"Why?"

"Because I knew if you left it you wouldn't want to come back."

"Well of course I wouldn't want to come back."

"Well, there you go."

"It doesn't solve anything for you to run off to another state."

"Yes it does. It kept you from leaving the house."

"Just like it doesn't solve anything for you to be drunk. In fact, it makes things worse."

"No it doesn't. It makes things better."

"To avoid your problems makes them better?"

"Sometimes when you're at a moment of crisis, the best thing you can do is become absent."

"So you deal with it later on."

"No. My point is, sometimes you skip the crisis, and when you come back, the problem's gone."

"Yes?"

"Because a lot of times, things seem like bad problems when they really aren't."

"Do you have an example?"

"I do. An example is, when Ken McInturff first got his truck, we were going to Wendy's and the air conditioner started thumping. We would have gone straight to the dealer, but we had to meet a building inspector right after lunch, so we went back to the site and met the inspector, and when we got back in the truck at three the AC was running as it should, and it's done so ever since. You see, if we had gone to the dealer that day straight from Wendy's it would have been a wasted afternoon. That's called sitting on a problem to see if it goes away, and it's done all the time."

"So that's why you came to Mississippi?"

"No, I came to Mississippi to help Dove deliver some furniture to his daughter."

"Does his daughter live at the Grand Cabochon Hotel?"

"She lives in Hattiesburg. And the other reason I came here is because you wouldn't answer the telephone when I tried to call you from Dove's. I got sick of hearing that damn machine and I started to wonder what the point was."

"The problems we have are not the kind that simply go away, Don. The problems are real."

"I assure you the problem with Ken's air conditioner was very real. It was thumping. We did not imagine it."

"But don't feel badly," she said, "because it's not like your coming here has made things worse. Staying would not have helped anything either. I don't think what's wrong can be fixed."

"Anything can be fixed," I said.

"No, not anything."

"Anything that somebody made can be fixed. The question is whether you want to fix it."

"That's beyond incorrect, but I'll let it go because it's not the point anyway. You don't think anything's wrong. You're contented."

"That's true, I'm contented now. We're eating in a restaurant, and I'm glad you're here."

She took a deep breath and turned away from me.

"Nothing has changed for me, as far as you're concerned," I said. "If anything, I like you more now than I ever did."

"That doesn't help, when you say that kind of thing," she said.

"I don't understand what you're saying."

"You won't admit anything's wrong," she said. "This leaves all of the weight on me."

"I don't get it."

"Every time you say you're happy and everything's good, I have to say no, we're sad and things are bad. It's all on me, just like it's all on me to drive to Mississippi in your ugly, broken-tape-player truck to pick you up out of a parking lot, Don. A parking lot. Do you see this?"

"Why do you have to say things are bad? Suppose you don't do that, and we say things are good?"

"It would work only if things were good. That isn't reality."

"We need to talk some more about reality," I said. "We need to come to an agreement on what it is."

"Yes we do."

"But not now."

"Right. Not now, because now I'm tired from driving twelve hours to collect you from a parking lot."

"Right."

She sat looking cross. I ate some of my cheeseburger. I guess it was the hangover or I don't know what, but something was causing me to salivate excessively.

She said, "By the way, what kind of weird message did you leave on your parents' answering machine?"

I had forgotten that. "Mom called?"

"She was helpful," Mary said. "I like your mother."

"She's good," I said. "What did you talk about?"

"A lot of really obvious stuff that you apparently have no clue of."

31

WE GOT A ROOM at the Manor View Motel in Gulfport, further down 90, across from the beach but several rungs down from the Grand Cabochon luxury-wise. I cleaned my foot but refused to show Mary the cut, which made her mad. She took a shower and got in bed with her hair wrapped in a towel, and then she went to sleep. I had drunk a great deal of iced tea at the restaurant, and for me, tea is far worse than coffee for keeping me awake. My head was better than before, but I was too alert to lie down. I watched television for a couple hours, and then I turned the sound up trying to wake Mary but she slept through it. I shook her by the shoulder but she waved me away. I found some paper in the drawer of the nightstand and started making a list, the first item of which was "Fix house," and then I got stuck. I would not know what fixing the house entailed until I could look at it. There was no point in quizzing Mary, who was famous for her imprecision in describing any sort of mechanical problem. The thought of our house and the mystery of its condition made me queasy again.

Time passed. I watched the digital clock on the nightstand. After ten I said, "Hey Mary."

"Stop pestering me," she said.

I sat quietly and a moment later she sat up in the bed squinting. The towel had come off her head, leaving her hair pressed flat on one side and projecting on the other. She said, "Why don't you go to bed?" She spoke in a high-pitched, vague tone that she has when she's not completely awake.

"I'm thinking about our house," I said.

She patted the nightstand for her glasses and put them on and then made a trip to the bathroom. When she came back to bed she turned on the lamp.

"Dove said you tried to quit drinking," she said. Her voice was back to normal now.

"I didn't try very hard."

"You're not drinking tonight, I see."

"I haven't got any beer. I may go out for some."

"It doesn't hurt you to take a break," she said. "I have a right to say this, since I drove here."

"You can say whatever you want to me. You have all rights. I was going crazy without you."

She considered. She said, "Do I want to be the thing you go crazy without?"

"It's an expression, Mary."

"Anyway, I'm not any help to you. You were already losing it before you left. What you need is to clean up, and just straighten up, and to stop drinking."

"Okay, I won't drink anymore," I said.

We looked at each other awhile and then she turned off the lamp and lay down again.

"Let's go out to the beach and have a walk," I said.

"No, I'm tired."

"It'll help you sleep better when we get back, though."

"Don't talk to me about my sleep, please. Does it occur to

you that the more we talk about my sleep, the harder it is for me to sleep? *Okay great,*" she said, and now she sat up and turned on the lamp again. "Now I'm awake. Thanks a lot."

"Come out for a stroll, then."

She put her face in her hands and made a growling, plaintive sound that was an expression of her frustration with me. Then she whipped the covers back and hurriedly put some clothes on. "Let's go, right now," she said. Pointlessly I felt a stab of lust for her.

It was still hot outside. The air was somewhat cooler than before, but you could feel the radiant warmth from the asphalt. I followed Mary directly across the lot and between some juniper bushes in a strip of landscaping. She wanted to cross 90 there but I coaxed her down to the light, where it was safer. We waited and crossed with the signal.

"Here we are," she said when we stopped on the concrete above the sand. We looked down at the beach and black water.

She said, "Do you want to go down, or can we just stand here and look?"

"Let's go on down," I said.

"You'll get sand in your cut."

"I'm not worried about that. It's not bad."

We stepped down through the loose, dry sand and onto the wet, hard part. There was enough light from the partial moon and from the highway that we could see fairly well. We came upon a small black case in the sand. It was the size of a shoe box, or a little longer, and it had a handle.

"What is that?" Mary said.

"I don't know."

I knelt and opened it up, and there was a clarinet inside.

"It's a clarinet," I said.

She knelt too and picked up one of the pieces out of the case. There were five pieces. The horn itself was black, made of wood, and the keys appeared to be nickel-plated. A normal clarinet, as far as I know.

"Did it wash up here?"

"It looks to me like somebody left it," I said.

"I wonder if they're coming back."

"Maybe so, when they notice it missing."

She set the piece back into its velvet hollow. The velvet was purple, I think, though I could not tell certainly in that light. There was a space along the front edge of the case which held a folded piece of rag and a tin of aspirin. I looked around to see whether someone might be watching us.

"Should we take it?" Mary said.

"I don't really want a clarinet," I said.

"Me neither."

We closed the case and left it in the sand, a little further up the beach in case the tide came in before someone recovered it. We walked on and Mary told me she was worried about me. I asked her why and she started listing things, most of them obvious, but then she added, "Talking out loud to yourself when other people can hear."

"When was I doing that?"

She said Dove had told her that on the phone.

"I wasn't talking to myself," I said.

"He said you were."

"How does he know who I was talking to?"

She took hold of my hand and we walked that way for a minute before letting go. I told her I wished we had a child, because if we did, maybe none of this recent badness would have happened.

"You wouldn't have lost your job if we had a child?"

"I don't think so. It would have given me something to focus on."

"Do you think you wouldn't drink if we had a child?"

"I don't know."

"Because if that were the case, instead of going to meetings, every drunk could take on an orphan."

A pack of bikers went by on the highway making a ruckus with their loud motorcycles. There was a breeze coming off the water now, not a cool one but it helped. I wasn't dripping with sweat. The lights along Highway 90 were a pinkish-orange color, curving off in both directions along the coast. On the water one vessel was lit up in the distance. Some rich people maybe, having cocktails late? Or maybe there was fishing or shrimping at night. As I continued to look I saw other boats, not just the one.

"Time to head back," Mary said. She took my arm and pulled me around to face the way we'd come.

"Easy. I've got a bad foot," I said.

"Is it bad or is it not bad?" She faced me with her hands on her hips and her head held up. Her side towards the highway was lit so that I saw her skin and the outline of her new haircut. "Your limp keeps going away and coming back. Are you pretending?"

"No I'm not pretending."

"Just be like you are," she said.

I suggested to her that we might view Dove's twenty-three thousand dollars as a loan. We could go back to Tennessee and buy ourselves a new house with central heating and air.

"This is not the way intelligent people decide things," she said.

"I'm not intelligent, so I decide things however I can."

"I don't want to buy a new house, Don. I'm not even sure where I'll be in a month."

"What do you mean, where you'll be?"

"I applied for a job in Knoxville."

After considering this new information I said, "We could buy a house in Knoxville, then."

She didn't answer but stood looking at me. I said, "Why are you looking at me that way?"

"What way?"

"Like I'm a dog about to be euthanized. Is there any more bad news?"

"No. That's it."

"Are you going to get this job?"

"Probably not. But I might apply for others."

"Well that's fine," I said. I deliberately adjusted the pitch of my voice, sounding calm. "Look, it's over. You don't have to feel badly about it. I'll get a lawyer. We'll divide our liabilities. What the hell kind of job is it, anyway?"

"Event coordinator."

"What is that?"

"It pays well."

"That's great, Mary. I'll be happy for you."

"Okay. Enough."

"Really," I said.

"All right. Let's walk."

I asked her if she was hungry.

"More tired than hungry, now."

"Okay."

She put her arm around me and gave me a slight squeeze, which I'm afraid I didn't take very well, bending away almost involuntarily. We passed the clarinet again and returned to the Manor View.

32

ONCE MORE I WAS WITHOUT clean undergarments, so back at the room I had laundry day and washed my socks, shorts, and shirt in the sink and then hung them from the shower-curtain rod with the heat lamp on in the ceiling. Mary went back to sleep and then I also got to bed. I finally dropped off, I would calculate, around five. I woke up at nine to find Mary already up and dressed. I pulled myself together and we hit the road with me driving.

"Do you have the money?" she said.

I didn't have it. I had put it in the drawer of the nightstand when we went out for our beach walk. U-turns were prohibited, so I turned right, then right, and then I circled in a parking lot, and then I turned left, then left back onto 90. I sped a tenth of a mile and turned left into the Manor View parking lot and hopped out of the truck and went to the front desk, where I asked to please be let into the room I had checked out of because I had left some important family pictures in the nightstand. After waiting some minutes I was accompanied by the desk clerk up the sidewalk to the room. There we found

Mary with the cleaner, both of them irritated with me. Mary had the envelope. We left a second time.

"Let's get this money back to Dove now," Mary said.

"He won't take it, the old bastard."

"You're too rough on him."

"He said he never wanted to see me again."

"Let's get it in a bank, then."

I said, "Let's give it to his daughter. She can figure out what to do with it."

"Is that what Dove would want?"

"I don't know what Dove wants. The last thing I knew of that Dove wanted was to never see me again."

We rode north out of Gulfport, past the Taco Sombrero with its nice burritos and Budweisers and CLOSED sign on the door. "I don't know," Mary said. "I thought Dove didn't get along with his daughter now."

"Who does he get along with?"

"So you put the money in a bank, where it's safe."

"Dove doesn't believe in banks." Then I considered further and added, "If I put it in a bank, I'll have to come back down here and withdraw it for him later."

"They have ways of doing that electronically."

"I have other things to think about now. I want to wash my hands of Dove."

We left the open beachy country and came back into the pine-tree woods. There were hardwoods also, but the pines were what made the impression, with their aura of dinosaur country. Though they're green all year, pines don't convey lushness. We passed the town of Wiggins, Mississippi and a good-sized sawmill operation there, and I smelled the piney smell and thought of other things that I associate with pines, like cones, needles, and starter wood. I thought about our King wood-and-coal stove in our house in Gray, and about my long-time apprehensiveness concerning wood heat and house fires in general. I've been assured that wood heat is not dangerous if the flue is kept clean and in good repair. More house fires are caused by electrical faults than by anything else, if you believe the newspapers. Most electrical faults are the result of unsound practices on the part of the homeowner, such as using a cheap sixteen-gauge extension cord with a space heater.

I questioned Mary again about the electrical fault that had resulted from the truck running into our house. Did the breaker trip at the moment the truck hit, or later? Was there blinking or dimming of lights in any other area of the house? Her answers were vague. Had she smelled a burning smell?

"I smelled a log truck," she said.

"Sarcasm gets us nowhere," I said.

"You'll have to look at the house yourself."

"If you had spoken to me before you left, I would have told you to switch the main breaker off."

"According to Dove, you were too busy hunting for a liquor store to talk to me."

"We know I'm bad," I said. "That's not the topic. I'm trying to understand what condition our house is in."

"Why?"

"So I'll know the kind of project I'm in for, when I get home."

"It's off the foundation," she said.

"I suppose you just now remembered that minor detail."

We rode in quietness. In another forty-five minutes we were at the green drive-in theater outside Hattiesburg, and I turned.

"Where are we going?" Mary asked.

"To Rhonda's. I thought we decided to give her the money."

"I didn't decide that."

"Well, we're here, anyway."

We weren't quite there, but I found the way. I parked at the end of the yard beneath some trees. Rhonda's Mustang wasn't around. "It looks like no one's home," Mary said.

"We'll try anyway," I said. I took the envelope with me and knocked at the front door. Nothing stirred. I waited a moment and tried the knob. The door was locked. I rattled it good and cursed.

I decided I wasn't keeping this money, even if I had to smash a window to get in and leave it. I was confident I could find a way in without breaking things, though. I came down off the porch and crossed some monkey grass and parted two sloppy azalea bushes that were as tall as my head. I was squeezed in there up against the house wrestling with a window screen when a white LeSabre pulled into the yard, followed by a blue van. A woman got out of the LeSabre and came up onto the porch and knocked on the door. I said hello to her and she looked past me until I said, "I'm here in the bush."

She came to the edge of the porch and peered at me. "Good afternoon, Mr. MacPherson," she said.

I told her I wasn't Mr. MacPherson.

"Is this his residence?"

"Yes, but he isn't here."

"Can you tell me when he will be back?"

"No I can't," I said.

She was a rather short lady in her fifties or so. She was holding a briefcase. She stood looking at me. "I'm not a bill collector," she said.

"I'm not Jimbo MacPherson," I said.

"If you are, you should say so, because I have something good for him."

"What would that be?"

"I'm sorry, but I can only tell Mr. MacPherson."

"Oh well," I said, and she said she would try back in a couple of hours. She left, along with the van. I got the screen off to find the window locked. I came out from the bushes and went back to the truck. I gave the envelope to Mary and told her the lady had something good for Jimbo. Mary asked me why I had gone into the bushes.

"To go in through the window," I said.

"This is getting stupider and stupider," Mary said.

I was in the driver's seat with my door standing open for some air. I had intended to go back and check some more windows, but I didn't feel like getting up. Mary was sitting sideways with her back against the door and her bare knee on the seat. Her arm was along the seat back. The envelope was in her lap. She opened it and took a rubber-banded stack of bills out and sniffed at it.

"It's got a certain smell," I said.

She nodded once, frowned, and put the money away in her purse. I saw that she was crying, which shocked me. She doesn't cry often, and I had not seen this one coming. When she saw that I had noticed she batted her hand at me and turned her head away towards the window. After a second she wiped her eyes. "What kind of hostile world is this?" she said.

I told her I didn't think it was a hostile world.

"Maybe yours isn't," she said.

I told her I lived in the same world that she did.

"You're not barren," she said.

I had never heard her say such a thing before. It occurred to me that I had possibly brought this on with my talk on the beach of how things might have been different, had we had a baby. I told her that I thought we should never use the word "barren," but if we did it would apply more to me than to her.

"There's nothing wrong with you," she said.

"I mean because I'm floundering and don't have a job," I said. "You're productive and smart and responsible."

She stared at me quietly. I looked at her damp face and then her throat and arms, thinking that she was beautiful but not wanting to say it because I thought it would make things worse. But then I couldn't stop myself, and I said it. She shrugged.

I said, "I don't think we're barren, because we sort of did have a baby."

She looked away from me towards the dashboard. She didn't say anything, but I had an idea what she might be thinking. It was important that I go slowly now. I didn't want to screw this up.

"I want you to suppose something," I said. "Look here. First off, I'm here now, right?"

"You're there," she said.

"Right. And you're talking to me, correct?"

"I am talking to you."

"But how do you know I'm really here?"

She didn't say anything to that.

I asked her had she ever heard of a person talking to plants.

"The prince of Wales," she said.

"Right! He's a prince, and he does that."

"So what?"

"Well, leave that there for a minute and let me ask you this. You talk to the dog sometimes. Does he understand you?"

"Yes."

"How do you know?"

"I tell him to come get his supper, and he comes and gets his supper."

"But you also tell him things like hello and goodbye," I said. "You tell him hello when you walk in the door, and you tell him goodbye when you leave. You never tell him hello when you leave."

"Hello?"

"So you're talking to the dog, when you do that. All right, now let's look at one other thing. Did it ever occur to you as a possibility that another person, like your mother for example, might be a robot?"

"No it didn't."

"It did to me," I said. "Because how would you know?"

"My mother's not a robot."

"I'm not saying she is. I'm saying how do you know it?"

"You'd know it, Don. Robots don't sneeze."

"One could be programmed to sneeze."

"This is sounding psychotic. Are you confused? Do you see robots?"

"No I don't. That's my point."

"You've lost me, then. Why are you talking about my mother?"

"I'm not only talking about her. It could be anyone's mother."

"Do robots have mothers?"

"No, they don't. What I'm saying is, in the course of growing up, a normal thing that a person might wonder is, What if my parents are robots? Suppose my whole family is an experiment, and my parents are not really inside their bodies but are machines that are observing me? That's possible, and what occurs to people is that there's no way to prove it isn't the case."

"I don't agree that that's a normal thing to wonder."

"Gather the point, though."

"I don't see the point," she said.

"The point is that you never know what a person is thinking, or even that they are thinking anything. A person's mind could be a total blank, and the person is just walking around making facial expressions and saying things that are sort of appropriate. Do you admit that's possible?"

"No."

"Well, it is possible. But nobody believes it."

"Crazy people believe it."

"Right. But sane people believe that they are not alone. They believe that there are other minds around them. And that's an example of believing in something you can't see."

"But the dog looks at me, Don. He's there, he comes when I call, he smells me. This other thing you're talking about is not here. It does us no good if it's not here."

"How do you know it's not here?" I said.

"I can't see it. That's how I know."

She had a point. I had one too, or I had had one. I had thought so.

"What if it isn't here?" I said. "It could be somewhere else."

"Where?"

"Someplace different," I said. "I don't know where." I looked around us—the street, the beat-up yard, the pines we were parked under, the hot whitish sky. I looked at my arm, and there was a tick on it. I jumped a little and then froze. Mary is very phobic about ticks, so I didn't want her to know of it. Fortunately it wasn't attached yet so I unobtrusively flicked it out the door and then I pushed my fingers through my hair several times and around my neck.

"Let's go," Mary said.

"Okay. Let me check the oil first," I said. I hopped out of the truck and raised the hood and then stood in front of it out of her sight and pulled off my shirt and shook it out. I didn't find any more ticks. I then put my shirt back on and checked the oil level. It was fine.

I got back behind the wheel and cranked the engine. "I guess this money's going in the bank after all," I said. "I know I'm not climbing through any more bushes."

"Wait, Don," she said. She grabbed my arm.

"What?"

I looked at her, and then I looked where she was looking.

The front door of the house was standing open.

"How did that get open?" I said.

Then I looked again and saw Michael standing at the bottom of the porch steps.

33

HE WAS HOLDING A SPATULA. As we walked towards him he squatted on the dirt in front of the steps and started jabbing the ground with the handle of it.

"Hello Michael," I said. "What are you doing?"

He looked up at me and then at Mary, who was behind me.

"You're using that spatula wrong," I said.

He flipped the spatula and began scraping the dirt with the flat part, as though he was frying bacon. The kid had a wit, in his manner. Mary stepped up to him and leaned forward with her left hand on her knee, her purse hanging behind her arm. She said, "Michael?" When he didn't look at her she took another step and in a move I found very beautiful knelt near him, at the same time pulling some hair away from her face and tucking it behind her ear—something she normally does only when she believes no one is looking, because she thinks it looks bad tucked behind her ear. I like it that way. With the curls it tucked even better.

I asked Michael whether anyone was home.

Mary said, "Every child knows not to answer that question, Don."

"His name's not Don," Michael said.

I said, "Let's go inside."

"Why don't you check in there first?" Mary said.

"What for?"

Mary turned so Michael couldn't see her face, and she mouthed the words "Check the house."

I did as I was told. I didn't expect to find anything wrong, but the suspense of opening doors made me so edgy that when I looked in the back bedroom I thought I saw Jimbo's blown-up corpse lying facedown in the carpet. It was only a long mound of laundry.

When I came back out to give Mary the all-clear, Michael was questioning her about her connection to me. Was she my wife? Where had she been? Were we divorced? His face was smudged, and Mary asked me to get a paper towel from inside. I did this and thought to dampen it as well, and Mary wiped his face with it. He endured the wiping without more than a pause in the interrogation. It was part of his daily drill to have a woman wipe his face.

"Where do you live?" he asked Mary.

"In Tennessee."

"Do you know my grandfather?"

"Yes."

"Is he coming here?"

"I don't know."

I interrupted to ask Michael when he expected one of his parents back.

He shrugged. He asked whether we were hungry.

"No thank you," Mary said. "Are you?"

"I ate," he said.

I asked Mary what she wanted to do.

She asked Michael, "Do you know where I can reach your mother? Do you know the phone number?"

He didn't have an answer.

"Do you have a phone number where I can call your father?" she said.

He gave Mary a phone number, and I went in and called it and got a recording saying "You have dialed another party on your line." I didn't know what that meant, so I hung up. Then the phone rang. I picked it up and said hello, and nobody answered, and then I realized I had called myself. I hung up on myself and went back outside. I told Mary I guessed we would have to wait with Michael until someone came home.

She simply nodded and did not say anything. She and Michael were sitting together on the front steps, and I studied them and let sink into my head some of the possible things that Mary might be thinking or feeling. Only she knew. At any rate I was fed up with Rhonda and Jimbo. Mary listened to Michael calmly. She appeared steady and strong, and I guessed that it was because she had made up her mind to be that way. I was impressed and proud of her, though at the same time it seemed to me an injustice that a person as good as Mary should have to make herself be brave at any time.

A half hour passed. Michael got up and moved around, smacking things with his spatula. He had energy and couldn't rest. I asked Mary if she would not prefer to go inside the house and find some toys to occupy him, and she said, "Not really," in a tone which suggested to me that she wanted as little to do with the house as possible. I didn't blame her, with the musty smell wafting out the open front door.

I was getting restless and twitchy myself. I proposed we go into the woods and look for arrowheads.

"We need to stay up front," Mary said.

But Michael had heard me and he became fixed on the idea. Mary told him no, and he pulled on the cuff of her shorts. Like his father, he had a weak sense of personal boundaries. He was very insistent, and then I made the mistake of saying to Mary, "What would it hurt?" which Michael repeated. He was like a little mob. He pleaded and tugged until Mary stood up and let him lead her around the side of the house. I followed.

"If you do see an arrowhead, don't pick it up," I said.

"Why not?" Mary said, and I told her about Jimbo's patented patina-making process. She said she didn't believe it.

"I'm not saying it works," I said.

She had Michael by the wrist and he pulled her into the woods the same way we had gone before. There wasn't a path really. The pines were dense enough that their shade kept the brush from taking over and you could walk among them on the bed of needles, which was springy with an occasional crunch of a twig.

We looked for snakes. We found a turtle shell with some bones inside it, and we found a mattress. How a mattress makes its way into the woods I don't know, but it was not the first time I had come across one in this kind of setting. We found a perfect climbing tree and I told Michael to run up it. He looked at me as though I was a stranger.

"When I was your age I would have got to the very highest reaches of that tree in fifteen seconds," I said.

Mary said, "Don't tell him to do that."

"Do we not climb trees anymore? Is that over and done with?"

"He's too small," she said.

Michael looked up towards the tree now. It was a maple

tree, I think. He set his spatula down. I lifted him up and set him in the lowest branch, which was huge and almost horizontal, and he seemed to like it. He growled. He climbed up another few branches, past where I could reach him.

"Come down now," Mary said.

Looking at him, I decided that perhaps I had been somewhat older than six when I used to climb trees a lot. He was up pretty high. I asked him to come down and he said he was scared to.

I told him that climbing up the tree was only half the job. He opened his mouth very wide, as though he was going to scream, but nothing came out. He held up his hand and flung a big brown roach off of it. He began to sniffle and whimper.

"Okay, I screwed up," I said. I turned to see Mary. "Now what?"

"Boost me up," Mary said. She handed me her purse and put her hands on the tree with her back to me.

"No, I'll do it," I said. "I'm the dumbass that put him up there."

"Just shut up and boost me," she said.

I got her onto the low branch, and then she stood up on it. She could reach his ankle. She said, "Okay, Michael. Nothing's wrong. This is a good tree." She smiled at him. He stopped his whimper and looked unhappily at the back of his hand, where the roach had been. "There's no rush, so let's relax a minute," she said.

"Yes, relax," I said. "That's a good idea. The roach is gone now." I stomped on the ground, pretending I had seen it and was killing it.

Mary asked Michael if he would reach down and give her his arm.

"Yes," he said, but he didn't do it.

"Why don't you give me your arm?" she said.

"In a minute," he said.

We waited. Mary wouldn't look at me. She had that brusque manner that she gets when she is deeply whizzed off at me. I had seen her this brusque many times, but never in a tree. She looked good up there on the branch with her strong white legs. I was in trouble again.

I asked her what I could do to help and she told me the only way I could help now was to be quiet. Just then we heard Michael's name being screamed from the direction of the house.

It was Rhonda. I hollered back to her and the yelling got closer, and then we heard sticks crunching and heard her heaving. She was in tears and badly frightened. She saw me first and ran up to me and had grabbed me by the arm before she even saw Mary. Then she saw Michael. She had been up at the house looking for him, and even up and down the street. She was wearing a dark red business suit complete with skirt, jacket, and silk blouse. Her hair was pulled back in an elaborate and dressy way. She had no shoes on.

She wiped her eyes with both hands and went to the tree. "Come down from there, Michael," she said.

"He's scared," Mary said.

To my surprise Rhonda reached both hands up her skirt and began working her panty hose off. When I understood what she was doing I turned my back. She got them off quickly and told me to give her a leg up. I made a stirrup with my hands and she stuck her foot in it and then she was up on the branch with Mary. In the process she kicked me in the eye with her heel. No one noticed that but me, and I didn't mention it.

I stepped back to look. Mary had edged down the branch and was holding to another branch over her head. She was a bit

taller than Rhonda, I noted. Rhonda said, "Come here, baby,"
but Michael would not go to her any better than he had gone
to Mary. I decided he was playing with us now. I didn't say so
because it would have meant death to me at that moment by
having a woman jump out of a tree on me. But I saw that the
sniffling had stopped. Old Michael was paying close attention
to these two women. He was going to remember this rescue for
all of his days.

Rhonda tried to climb higher but because of her skirt,
which was fairly snug, she couldn't raise her leg. She had me go
stand under Michael in case he fell. Then she and Mary
changed places, and Mary climbed higher and got her arm
around his torso. I saw him quiver, and his feet straightened
out. Mary crouched and handed him down to Rhonda, who
squeezed him till his eyes popped and then handed him down
to me. I set him on the ground.

Rhonda came down off the branch and then Mary. It was
about a five-foot jump using me as a sort of handrail. When
they'd all landed, Mary introduced herself. Rhonda took
Michael by the shoulder and pulled him up against her legs,
and then she shook Mary's hand.

"I saw your truck in front but I didn't know whose it was,"
Rhonda said.

I told her we had been in the truck waiting for her when
Michael came out.

"He knows better than to come outside," Rhonda said. She
was talking to Mary. "I had a job interview, and it's hard to
find someone to stay with him."

Mary nodded. Michael leaned into his mother's legs.

"You must think I'm terrible," Rhonda said.

"We shouldn't have brought him back here," Mary said.
"I'm sorry we scared you."

"That was my fault," I said. I was ignored.

"I have a sitter lined up for next week," Rhonda said.

"Did you get the job?" Mary asked.

Rhonda said yes she had. It was a job at a mall selling pre-scription eyeglasses. It did not pay as well as the job she'd quit a month earlier, but she needed something right away.

Mary took her purse from me and gave Rhonda the enve-lope out of it. "This is from Dove," she said.

Rhonda stared into the envelope for a good while. I told her he'd sold his place in Tennessee and she said she already knew that. She asked why he had not brought the money himself.

"You told him to leave," I said.

"I had a reason," she said. "What does he want in return for this?"

"I guess nothing," I said. I looked to Mary for help. She was watching Rhonda.

"I don't believe that. He wants something," Rhonda said.

We started back towards the house. I'm not very quick at lying, and I wasn't sure how thick to pour it on. I said, "Dove's very sorry about what he did before. That thing about wanting Jimbo to leave."

Rhonda shot me a look over her shoulder, and Mary about knocked me down. I had forgotten I was speaking in front of the child.

"He's just sorry and he wants you to have it," I said.

Rhonda said, "Did he tell you he was sorry?"

"I heard him tell someone else that."

"Who did he tell that to?"

"This person named Nicole."

"Who's Nicole?" Rhonda said.

"A person we met in Biloxi," I said. "She's not important."

"Who is she?" Mary said.

"She's just this girl who took my knife," I said.

Unlikely as it may seem, I was very happy at that moment to see Jimbo arrive. We were coming back to the yard and he was rolling up on a ten-speed bicycle. He was wearing a clear plastic shower cap on his head.

Michael ran up and Jimbo lifted him, and then Jimbo propped his bike against the side of the house, and Rhonda gave him the envelope. Before opening it he looked Mary up and down and asked her if she was with me.

"Yes," Mary said. She smiled faintly and pushed her purse around behind her right elbow. I had seen her do this before when she was practicing her self-defense kicks.

Jimbo looked into the envelope. He asked whose money it was and Rhonda told him it was Dove's, and he asked why he was holding it, and Rhonda said Dove was giving it to them.

"I'm not accepting this," he said. He handed it back to Rhonda.

"This is a lot of money," Rhonda said.

"Twenty-three thousand dollars," I said.

"I don't need any handouts from that old crooked shank," Jimbo said. "I got a job."

I asked him what kind of a job it was.

"Supervisory," he said.

"You can tell that by his supervisory hat that he wears," Rhonda said.

Jimbo raised his hand to where he knew the top of his head to be and he felt for the cap, which he had evidently forgotten was there. "All right, I gut chickens. What thoughts do you have on that, Wendell?"

"I don't have any thoughts on that," I said.

"Maybe you'd enjoy making light of it."

"No. I wouldn't."

"And what do you do for a living, may I ask?"

"I'm unemployed," I said.

"You have my sympathy," he said to Mary. He heaved Michael onto his shoulders, and Michael pulled the plastic cap off his father's head and put it on his own. They went inside the house that way.

I told Rhonda if she didn't want to spend the money she could put it in a box, but we weren't carrying it around anymore.

She asked me where Dove was planning to live.

"Wherever he wants."

"Not with no money," she said.

I asked her had she heard about the qualifyings and how Jeff Gordon had done.

"He's on the pole," she said.

"Then Dove's got money." I explained about the bet at the hotel, including the amount.

Rhonda said, "Damn. What kind of bookie takes that size of bet?"

"An extremely tall, bald-headed one," I said.

Rhonda stood there staring, and then something caught her eye. She walked back to the edge of the yard and picked up her high-heeled shoes out of the grass.

"Let's go," Mary said. She nudged my arm. "Goodbye, Rhonda," she said.

"Goodbye," Rhonda said. She sniffed and looked at what she was holding—the shoes, her panty hose, a spatula, and an envelope of cash. "Thank you for staying with Michael," she said.

Mary smiled at her and we got in the truck and left. It was after two o'clock, and we had five hundred miles to drive. Neither one of us was happy now. We hadn't eaten any lunch, either.

We wound our way back out to U.S. 49. Mary asked me who did I think the man and woman were who had come in the white LeSabre and van. I had no idea and didn't care, I said. She told me the man's head was shaved and he was so tall he couldn't sit up straight in the van.

I thought about that. Mary and I looked at each other.

The next question was why Dove would send a bookie to Jimbo.

"To give Jimbo the money he won," Mary said.

"According to the lie I told Rhonda, he would. But according to reality, Dove would rather drive on top of Jimbo with a forklift."

Then I told Mary all I knew and had been holding back about Dove's original plan to shoot Jimbo, which was really why I was here, and also why Mary was here, because it was the real reason for the trip to begin with, though I hadn't known so. I also told her about Dove trying to pay Rhonda to leave Jimbo, and Dove's scuffle with Jimbo at Gene's bar, and Jimbo's story that Dove had been in prison for shooting somebody, which, when I asked him about it, Dove had failed to deny. I told her about finding Dove in the bathtub with his pistol.

She asked me did I suppose that this man Dove had given fifteen thousand dollars in cash to was not really a bookie.

"I'm starting to think he wasn't," I said.

"Pull over and we'll call the police," she said. There was a Shell station on the right that she pointed to. I pulled in.

"You can use the phone inside," she said.

"That'd cause a big ruckus in there," I said. "Me calling the police."

"Then go to the pay phone." She went into her purse for change.

"I'm not sure I want to do this," I said.

"Do what?"

"If I call the police, they'll come to the house, who knows what will happen, and then they'll put Dove in jail."

"Maybe Dove belongs in jail," she said.

"He's old," I said. "He's prone to rashness. He gave us all that money."

"You said he punched you in the head."

"That's his way. I want to go back and talk to those people."

"What people?"

"The lady and man. This can be settled somehow." I pulled out of the Shell lot and back onto 49, going south.

Mary stared at me and I was afraid to look at her. I was pretty damn sure this time what she was thinking and what was going to happen next. It could happen now or it could happen ten hours from now, or two weeks from now when she moved to Knoxville for her new job. We didn't speak. She faced out the window and at one point she laughed abruptly and then she was quiet again. We got back to Rhonda and Jimbo's and I stopped in the yard and got out and shut the door, and Mary moved to the driver's side and started the truck with her own key and left.

34

I SPOKE TO JIMBO and then he spoke to Rhonda, and she left with Michael in the Mustang. Jimbo went off down the hall and I sat on the couch regretting that I was there.

In a minute Jimbo came back up the hall with a shotgun in one hand, a clip pistol in the other hand, and a box of shells under his arm. He set the pistol on top of the television and looked for a place to put the box of shells. There was a large window at the front of the living room, and he looked out of it then pulled the curtains shut. He broke open the shotgun and loaded a shell in the barrel and set the box on the carpet. The top of the television was slanted and the pistol started to slide, and he stopped it. We stared at each other and then he asked me if I wanted a beer.

"No, and I don't want you to drink one either," I said.

He took his shotgun into the kitchen and I heard him crack a beer open. There was a pause and then I heard him smash the can.

"Let's try to have a plan," I said when he came back.

"First I'm going to protect my home," he said. "Then when

this is finished I'm going to Biloxi and wring her daddy out like a rag, and stop up the plumbing with him."

I told Jimbo I wouldn't be surprised if Dove had already accomplished that on his own by now.

Jimbo considered. "He's got you feeling sorry for him."

"He's alone," I said.

"Wonder why."

I said I thought it would be best for Jimbo to stay out of the way when the people came back. I would get a look at the man and find out if he was the one Dove gave the money to.

"And if he is?"

"I'll tell him you're not home yet."

"So he comes back tomorrow. Nothing is solved."

"Okay. I'll tell him something different," I said.

"What?" He was at the window with his shotgun, looking past the edge of the curtain.

"Let me think," I said.

"If you can't think it's not my fault," he said.

He sat down at the other end of the couch from me and fidgeted. He told me he had gutted ninety chickens today before he slit his finger, which was why he had come home before the end of the shift. He showed me the bandage on his left middle finger. He said, "My rate is not the fastest, but it's the fastest among new employees." Then he asked me in my opinion how many chicken lives were equivalent to one human life. I told him his question was nonsense and he said, "Do you think that the life of a chicken has any value whatsoever?"

"I suppose it does," I said.

"If it has some little bit of value, then the lives of two chickens have twice that value. If you add enough chickens together, the value will eventually come to an amount equivalent to the value of your own life."

"What has this got to do with anything?" I said.

"It's an example of something I think about. I'm thinking all the time."

I asked him where the money was.

"I can tell you where it's not."

"Look here," I said. "I can give them that money of Dove's to leave. He paid the guy fifteen thousand, but we've got twenty-three to offer."

"I like this idea," Jimbo said. "We pay them Dove's money to kill Dove."

"No, we're not paying them to kill Dove. We're paying them to not kill you."

He thought about it. "That's a lot of money to give away," he said.

"I don't intend to get shot for your sake," I said. "If somebody puts a gun on me and you're in there under the bed, I'm going to tell them you're in there under the bed."

"I can't fit under the bed. I've tried."

"Where is the money?"

"Rhonda had it."

"Well where did she put it?"

"I don't know."

"Well we need to find it!"

We both got up and started looking, and that's what we were doing when the van and LeSabre pulled into the yard again. Jimbo ran down the hall, taking both guns with him. I looked past the curtain and watched the woman come across the yard with her briefcase. She had short legs and a quick pace. At the wheel of the van, sure enough, was that same stooping seven-foot bald-headed man from the Grand Cabochon. I called down the hallway for Jimbo to keep looking for the money, and I went to the door.

"You just missed him," I told the woman. I looked down at her. She was wearing a yellow suit and a flowered blouse, and she had some perspiration under her eyes and over her lip. She didn't look nervous, only hot. I told her I had given Jimbo her message and he had told me to ask what it was about.

"I need to see him personally," she said.

"Who's that man in the van there?" I said.

"Just my driver," she said without looking back.

"Why is he coming over here, then?"

Now she looked. The man had unfolded himself from the van seat and was headed towards us, empty-handed. I came the rest of the way outside and shut the door behind me. The man had on the same gray pants and white shirt as the day before, or similar ones, and his bald head had a white stubble over the ears. "We've missed him again," the woman said.

The man came up the steps slowly and stood beside her, glowering at me.

There was a huffing from around the corner of the house, and Jimbo stopped in the front yard. He had his shotgun. He raised it at us and said, "Freeze. Put your hands up."

They raised their hands. The woman raised the briefcase.

"What's in that briefcase?" Jimbo said. He told me to take it from her, and she quickly handed it to me. "Look inside it," he said.

I asked the woman did she mind if I looked inside her briefcase.

"Do whatever he says!" she said.

I looked inside. It was only papers and Kleenex.

"Who are you?" Jimbo said.

"I'm an attorney," she said. "Are you Jimbo MacPherson?"

He made a big show of raising his thumb and pulling the

hammer back on the shotgun. I reached behind myself for the doorknob and found I had locked myself out.

"I represent Metropolitan Motors of Hattiesburg, and I'm here to offer a settlement to Jimbo MacPherson," the woman said.

"A settlement?" He lowered the shotgun. "What kind of settlement?"

"A final legal settlement of all your claims against my client," she said. She took back her briefcase and went down the steps and right up to Jimbo, waving a stack of pages at him. She was braver than I was. She said, "This is a legally binding settlement in which you relinquish all claims against the Metropolitan Motors Company of Hattiesburg in return for a consideration which you must agree never to reveal or discuss."

First he looked confused, and then Jimbo grinned. Then he stifled the grin and assumed an expression of grave concern, or tried to. He propped his gun against the porch and took the papers from the woman. The tall man and I came down off the porch.

"What's the consideration?" Jimbo said.

"This new Dodge Caravan," she said. She opened her hand towards it.

Jimbo looked at the van. "It's not what I'd have picked," he said.

"It's a wonderful van," the woman said. "I think you'll find it's a great family vehicle."

The tall man was staring at me. I looked at him and he shook his head as though he felt sorry about how dense I was.

Jimbo stepped over and peered in the passenger-side window. He tried the door and it was locked. "Other side," the tall man said. Jimbo nodded and walked around the front of the van and got in. He put his hands on the steering wheel.

I'm slow, but I was starting to get this one figured out. I apologized to the people about the shotgun. "We thought something else was going on," I said.

The lady smiled at me. "It got warm there for a minute," she said.

"If you mind your own business, you won't be minding mine," the tall man said.

Jimbo came back from the van and said the odometer was showing twelve hundred miles. "That's not new," he said.

"It's a demo," the woman said.

"I've driven a demo when I was a salesman and I was rough as hell on it," he said.

"This is our offer," she said.

Jimbo looked at me, and then he looked at the tall man. He asked me, "Is that the same guy you saw?"

I told him no, they were two different men.

Jimbo took the papers and signed where the woman showed him. She handed him a title and the tall man tossed him the keys, and then the couple left in their LeSabre.

Jimbo studied the key ring in his hand then dangled it for me to see. "One word," he said. "Vindication!"

He began a sort of touchdown dance in the yard, in the course of which he brushed against his shotgun, which he had not uncocked. It slid to the ground and went off pointing at the house. The noise was very loud, and I ran. The gun slid butt-first into the yard and stopped not far from where I had been standing.

Jimbo was still, and then he bent to look. Some monkey grass and part of an azalea were gone, and a couple of cinder blocks were shattered. He let out a whoop.

It was a rental house, so what did he care? I started walking.

"Let's go for a ride up the street," Jimbo said.

I told him no thanks.

"Can I drop you somewhere in my new van?"

"Walking suits me fine," I said. I crossed the road to Gene's, where the parking lot contained the brown Lincoln, Gene's I presumed, and a late-model Chevy pickup the color of cantaloupe flesh. I went in and Gene said, "Who's shooting?"

"Pea Brain across the street," I said. I started for a booth and there was Dove, sitting by the window flicking his lighter. My ear started to throb.

"Come set down and let's make up, Wendell," he said.

"I don't want to make up," I said.

"Get you a beer out of that cooler and bring it over here."

The thing was, I didn't have any cash on me. If Dove was buying then I couldn't afford to be proud. I went to the cooler.

"Get two," he said.

I did it, and joined him. He asked me what I was doing back at the MacPherson residence. I told him it was his fault but I didn't want to talk about it. He asked me where Mary was. "She left, and I don't blame her," I said.

"I don't blame her either but I blame you for letting her leave," he said.

I told him the reason she left was that I had come back here because of his stupid scheme. "What stupid scheme?" he said, and I said, "This stupid business with that van," and he said, "I don't know what you're talking about," and I said, "Yes you damn well do," and I explained the details to him and he admitted that yes, there had been no bet on Jeff Gordon, whom I should have known he would never bet on, and yes, he had bought the van and had the people pretend it was a "settlement," but I was the only one who knew the whole story, and if Ken McInturff or Walter Furlong ever found out that he had bought his dumbass son-in-law a Dodge Caravan he would know I was the one who told them. And he hoped I never would.

"I don't see why you choose to make things so complicated," I said.

"I'm not the one that pulled a shotgun on that small lady."

"If you'd simply given Jimbo the van, that would have been avoided," I said.

"If I had just give him the van he wouldn't have took it."

I told him he was right, and the reason I knew was that I had tried to give Jimbo and Rhonda his money.

"I give you that money," he said.

"And I gave it to them, and Jimbo wouldn't take it," I said. But I added that I had a suspicion Rhonda had carried it with her when she left, to put in the bank.

"Not today she ain't, because it's Saturday," Dove said.

"I don't know what day it is," I said. I swallowed some beer.

Jimbo had driven off, and now Rhonda's Mustang pulled into the yard. She sat in it with Michael as though she was waiting for someone to come out of the house.

"She's afraid to go in," I said.

Dove asked why, and I explained that we had all believed the tall man and short woman were hired killers he had sent for Jimbo.

"I never did *that*," he said.

"Well, go tell her," I said.

He said no, he was only there to see that the van got delivered. I said okay, I would go tell her everything myself, and then I was going to call Walter Furlong and tell him the story of how Jimbo MacPherson got fired but it was all right because Dove Ellender bought him a new van free and clear, and Dove said, "Oh go to hell," and pushed himself up out of the booth seat and started scuffling towards the front to pay

Gene. It occurred to me that I had not seen his truck, and I asked him how he had gotten there.

"In my new truck," he said. He nodded towards the parking lot. "I had to have air-conditioning."

"But Rhonda has all your money," I said.

"Evidently not," he said.

I watched him cross the road, then pulled shut the curtain. Soon Jimbo would be back and there would be more touch-down dancing, and I didn't have the stomach to watch it. It wasn't his happiness that I objected to so much as the idea that he partly deserved it, with his gutting chickens to pay the rent and all that. I in contrast had come five hundred miles to avoid certain domestic responsibilities. In this I was no better than he was but actually worse. It was disappointing to think that a Jimbo could figure these things out quicker than I could.

I considered. I was not in a good spot, and the part I expected to be the most painful in the very near future was the thought of my having believed, for a while, that there was something permanent holding Mary and me together—a thing we had made that could not be disregarded no matter how much we tried not to talk or even think about it. It was something I was reluctant to put a name on, though I badly wanted it to be real. This thing—you know who you are.

But if almost making you was not enough, and you aren't quite fully real, then my fondness for you is also not real. Or else it is a joke, which makes me a joke as well. The reason it makes me a joke is that I am slightly over six feet tall but a mere child in my insistence on believing what suits me and serves my wishes, as opposed to what is the case in the world.

I sat for a long time, and then I thought, What the hell? If truly what I see is all there is, and there is no perfect world somewhere else where our love and its objects can be protected from accidents and stupidity, then the thing to do is to seek consolations. Consolations do exist, and in fact there was a whole chest-type cooler of them at the front of this very room. Some could be mine if I could only find a way.

I thought hard, and then I had another idea. I said, "Hey Gene. How would you like for me to wash your car?"

A slow-metabolism person, he didn't react immediately. His white-haired head drooped, and then he turned it towards me and raised two fingers. He knew what I was getting at, because he had certainly heard such offers before. Whatever his answer, I was confident it would be fair.

At the same time as I was waiting to learn whether I was going to get another beer or not, the door creaked open and Mary stepped in. She looked around her at the room and saw me. "Come on and let's go back to Tennessee," she said.

I have never got up from a booth seat quicker. I gave Gene a parting salute and Mary and I got in the truck with her at the wheel and we left Hattiesburg behind us.

"I'm glad you're alive!" Mary said.

"So am I!"

She had talked to the MacPhersons and Dove. Rhonda was having trouble accepting that the dealership would give Jimbo a van after firing him.

"Rhonda is right to be skeptical," I said.

"But Dove and Jimbo both say it's for real."

I had a thought that happily confused me for a second. "Just because a thing is good doesn't mean it can't be real," I said.

"And just because a thing can't be real doesn't mean it isn't good," Mary said.

We rode and listened to Johnny Rivers, rewinding "Mountain of Love" several times. It's a song that stands up to repeated listenings. Hours went by, and something happened which I can't explain and won't attempt to. But it got so good that around Tuscaloosa we pulled off to the side of the road to have physical contact with each other. It was dark and we both had coffee breath. The cars and semis whished by us and we turned off the headlights and turned on the emergency blinkers.

35

OUR HOUSE WAS IN VERY BAD CONDITION. The morning after we got home, in a fit of not knowing what else to do, I managed to knock the stuck front door open with my shoulder, at which point a square yard of Celotex fell from the ceiling and shattered on the living room floor like pie crust. Then the door would not close again.

The house was not off its foundation, as Mary had said, but it had moved. What happened was that this log truck, after swerving and pushing the backyard fence down, had run into the corner of the house at the dining room. It had knocked the entire house some number of inches northeast. The limestone blocks were still in place. If you stood at the foot of the backyard you could discern a slight deformation in the line of the roof. It was not immediately apparent, because the house had not been perfectly square to begin with. On pulling up floorboards in the kitchen and what remained of the dining room, I discovered that the doubled joist at the rear of the house had failed. Perhaps it would not have done so except for a further problem that I discovered upon poking at the joist with a screwdriver, which was that I could easily push the screwdriver into the wood almost an inch. There was extensive insect damage. I found no live insects, of course, since I had sprayed the house to the legal limit the same week we closed and several times since. That only meant that the damage had been there all along, a hidden spongy place in the foundation of our home.

Now there were decisions to make, and each one affected all the others. Mary's car was in the shop—would we buy her a new one, or have the engine rebuilt? On Wednesday she took my truck to Knoxville and interviewed for the event-coordinator job. What if she got it? How could she not? On Friday an insurance adjuster came out to the house and said, "I can't believe we insured this place to begin with."

"Do you want me to show you the papers?" I said.

"I've got the papers," he said. I followed him around the outside one time and then in. He went to where I'd pulled the floor up and began inserting his own pocket-sized screwdriver into the insect-damaged wood. When he had probed three times I told him he had probed enough.

He stood up with effort and dabbed at his brow, slouched, winced, and shook his head. He said, "You're not thinking you'll try to fix this, are you?"

"It's my house," I said. "Of course I'm going to fix it."

He went to his car and sat doing calculations for ten minutes, and then he came back with a figure that he said would more than likely cause him to be fired for its excessive generosity, but it would enable my wife and me to pay our mortgage off and start over clean.

"We're not starting over at all," I said.

"This house will never again be insurable," he said.

Then he left, and I mowed the lawn. I was sitting in the smooth cut grass when the phone rang. I ran to get it because I was expecting a call from the garage where Mary's car was. When I answered a man said, "Is Mrs. Brush there?"

"She's not here," I said.

"Who is this?" the person said.

"First tell me who you are," I said.

"I was involved in a truck accident at her house and I want to know if she's going to sue me."

"Are you the driver?"

"Yes."

"Would you blame her if she sued you?"

There was a pause, and then the man said, "Her dog bit me, and I'm losing pay."

I hung up and called the dog to the kitchen to give him a treat. He came at a walk. He was on in years and not the same dog he had once been, but he had made the effort when it counted. If we were out of treats I intended to fry him an egg. Then the phone rang again, and a small voice said hello and asked me who I was.

"Is this Michael?" I said.

"Yes. Is Mary home?"

"She's at work."

He asked for her work number. I gave him that, and then I asked him if he was all right. He said yes, and I asked him whether his parents were home. He said no and set the phone down. I waited half a minute, and then I yelled into the phone for him to pick it up again, and then the phone rattled and a voice that sounded like a fourteen-horsepower Briggs & Stratton engine with the muffler rusted off said, "Who is this?"

"Dove?"

"Hello Wendell," he said.

"How are you?"

"Not good at all. I bought a new window unit and Jimbo

put it in wrong, and some people's supposed to be coming and take it out and put it back right, and I'm waiting around here with a towel on my head in this heat and may die."

"Mississippi is hot," I said.

"I know it. How's your housing situation?"

"Not too good," I said. I told him the details.

He said, "Hey Wendell, that boy will sell you my house for a nominal price of a hundred dollars."

"What boy?" I said.

"The boy I sold my place to."

"Why? Did he find out it's haunted?"

"That house ain't haunted. What are you talking about?"

"I don't know. What are you talking about?"

"He's going to flatten that house and put a Food City there. But he told me he would sell it for a hundred dollars if someone would move it."

"I don't have money to hire a bunch of house movers," I said.

"So you borrow it from the bank."

"I don't like borrowing," I said.

"But you're getting a house for a hundred dollars."

"I don't know if Mary will want your house."

"I can't figure that part out for you," he said.

We hung up and I went back to the kitchen and gave the dog a dog biscuit. I examined the insect damage again. To me it was a painful and senseless waste, but to the insects it had been food. I got up and called Mary at the library and left a message. In a couple of minutes she called back. "Guess whom I just got off the phone with," she said.

"Michael?"

"No, the director of libraries. She heard I got offered the Knoxville job and they're giving me a promotion if I stay."

"When did you get offered the Knoxville job?"

"This morning. Didn't you get my message?"

"What message?"

"Is the light blinking on the machine?"

It was blinking, only I hadn't seen it because there was a tape measure sitting on top of it. Not only was there a message from Mary saying she had been offered the Knoxville job, but there was also a message from the mechanic saying that the loss of oil pressure was due to a mysterious crease in the oil pan which he could not explain, but which he could repair for forty dollars.

This run of good luck concerned me. What was happening? That evening we drove by Dove's and let ourselves in with a key from above the back door. We walked through the house with a flashlight studying the floors and walls and trying to imagine ourselves living there.

"I like the molding at the ceilings," Mary said.

"The whole place stinks of cigarettes," I said.

"Some paint will fix that problem. We can also redo the kitchen."

"I guess we could," I said.

"Would that be hard?"

"No. It's the other part that's hard."

"You mean giving up on our house."

"Giving up on a lot of things."

She took the flashlight from me and shone it in my face.

"I can't see when you do that," I said.

We were in the bathroom, and she turned the light towards the mirror so we could both see both of us. "The only thing we're giving up on is our house," she said. "On all other things we're hopeful."

Then we knew what we had to do. There are three ways to take down a house that I know of: the first is board by board with crowbars and makes sense when the materials have salvage value, which the ones in our house did not. The second is with a bulldozer, which is fine but also requires the further step of hauling away the debris. The third is burning, and it is not permitted in all states or localities but it is permitted in Washington County, Tennessee so long as you notify the fire department ahead of time. I did this and a fireman came out and looked the place over, and I told him when we were planning to do it and he wrote down the date on a piece of paper I gave him and put it in his shirt pocket. I also called the power board and a storage company, and then I began to strip the house. Ken McInturff helped us move the furniture, and I saved some lighting fixtures and some of the windows, and one door, and some fairly new plywood from upstairs, and the sinks and tub. I made four trips to the dump, and I gave the man there his computer cables, which he told me he had been impatient to have.

Then on a Tuesday morning George Massey and Ken came over early, and we burned down the house. Well, first we had some coffee in the front yard. It was misty and there was dew on the grass. We tied up the dog and made sure the cat was out of the way. Then I went in the house and pulled up some more boards from the dining room floor, and I stacked them upright on the porch and splashed kerosene over them. I had already set a can or jug of kerosene in every room. If you pour it out, it evaporates.

"Who's going to light her up?" George said.

Ken gave a quiet, short laugh.

"I'll do it," Mary said.

She had called in sick for the occasion. Now she walked out to the road and took from its box the *Johnson City Press*, which had just arrived. She pulled out the classifieds and wadded a page. She was businesslike, moving quickly—my fine, brave Mary. Then she lit the wad of paper with a match and tossed it onto the pile of wood and ran back and grabbed my hand.

About the Author

JAMES WHORTON, JR. was raised in Florida and Mississippi and educated at the University of Southern Mississippi and Johns Hopkins. He lives with his wife in Washington County, Tennessee.

Printed in the United States
By Bookmasters